THE CLATTER MAN

JANELLE SCHIECKE

Emerald Link Press

Copyright © 2025 by Janelle Schiecke

All rights reserved.

No part of this publication may be reproduced, distributed, or transmitted in any form or by any means, including photocopying, recording, or other electronic or mechanical methods, without the prior written permission of the publisher, except as permitted by U.S. copyright law. For permission requests, visit www.janelleschiecke.com.

The story, all names, characters, and incidents portrayed in this production are fictitious. No identification with actual persons (living or deceased), places, buildings, and products is intended or should be inferred.

Book Cover by Jelena Gajic

To my husband and son, the loves of my life.
To Steph and Desiree—thank you so much for your love, support, and friendship.
And to my brother, Bryan, who has a heart of gold and unwavering determination.

Love will have its sacrifices. No sacrifice without blood.

                                        J. Sheridan Le Fanu

CONTENTS

Prologue		1
1.	Spook	7
2.	Beginnings	17
3.	A Warm Departure	23
4.	Chill	27
5.	Abby's Darkness	31
6.	Let's Get Lit	37
7.	Reeves Cabin	45
8.	To Friendship	51
9.	Campfire Stories	55
10.	The Clatter Man	61
11.	Fun and Games	71
12.	Second Thoughts	77

13.	Night Scares	81
14.	Presence	87
15.	I Got a Bad Feeling	91
16.	Hot and Bothered	99
17.	Rude Awakening	105
18.	Lights Out	111
19.	A Bump in the Road	119
20.	Instinct	125
21.	Mad Dash	131
22.	Flicker	139
23.	Clash	145
24.	Dark Lucidity	151
25.	Finding Solace	157
26.	At Last	163
27.	Against All Odds	169
28.	Forlorn	175
	Epilogue	181
	Afterword	187

Also by	195
About the author	197

PROLOGUE

Shelley scrambled to turn the doorknob, looking behind her shoulder after each attempt to make sure it wasn't approaching. Her blood-soaked fingers glided over the fixture as if performing some sick dance, and she just couldn't get a firm grip. "C'mon... c'mon!"

Grabbing it with both hands, she tried with all her might, but the knob wouldn't budge. David looked up at her with questioning eyes full of innocence only a six-year-old could possess. He pursed his lips and then cocked his head, confusion written all over that precious face. She'd been babysitting him for a year, and how she would explain this night to his parents was the least of her worries right now.

First, they had to get out of here alive.

It occurred to her horror-stricken mind in a moment of clarity that wiping wet hands on fabric tends to dry them. Rubbing her hands on her jean shorts did the job; then she grabbed the bottom of her T-shirt, using the fabric to remove the doorknob of any residual blood. For a split second, she registered how deadly quiet the house was now. The family dog could still be heard barking upstairs... upstairs where her boyfriend's corpse now lay. Her lips quivered as she thought of how easily the soft flesh of his throat had yielded to the sharp, steel blade. And that sound... that horrific gurgling sound as his life spilled out deep red from the gaping slit.

"Miss Shelley?" David tugged at her T-shirt. "What's going *on*?"

"Shh!" She pressed her pointer finger against her lips and gently turned the doorknob now with her other hand, welcoming a soft, warm spring breeze against her skin as the front door creaked open.

"But what about Max?" he pleaded as she scooped him up in her arms and ran to her car.

"Max... Oh, sweetie. Max will be okay," Shelley managed to mumble as the gravel snarled under her pounding footfalls and her chest burned with each frantic inhale.

When they reached her car, she placed David down and fished for her keys. Her keys that she realized were in her purse, which was in the house. A lump formed in Shelley's throat as she looked up now at the front visage of the residence, every muscle in her body stiffening for fight or flight. But flight was no longer an option.

The melody of crickets against the midnight sky swelled now to a maddening rhythm, and she winced as a pang of defeat flared in her chest. Somehow Max was still barking inside, and suddenly this all seemed like a bad dream she would wake up from. But as the large figure stepped through the open front door, stark reality set in again and she froze, unsure of what to do next. All she could hear now was her own breathing and David's sweet voice, muffled as if underwater, asking, "Who is that?"

Looking to her left, she saw the soft amber glow of the front porch light from the Warrens' house. The Warrens were a nice elderly couple; they could help, they had a phone. She'd have to run like their lives depended on it, though—and this time they really did.

Scooping David up in her arms again, Shelley turned on her step and began racing to the Warrens' house. Every so often she'd turn to look behind her, but the figure was gone. Puzzlement and hope worked their way across her brow as the neighbor's house became closer with each swift stride.

This nightmare would soon be over; safety was in sight.

But she could hear something else now... something skittering in the dark peripheral. As a petrifying realization set in, an electric surge ignited within her body and all feeling in her legs practically dissipated as she gained even more momentum. David's body was warm against hers, and his small head nestled in the crook of her neck. Little arms were wrapped tightly around her, with tiny fingers that fidgeted nervously along her neckline.

"Don't worry, Davey," she cooed under her breath. "It's almost over."

Searing pain erupted in Shelley's calf now, and she was pulled backward as David tumbled from her arms. Stars burst into her vision as the side of her skull crashed hard against the ground. David's harrowing screams kept her from slipping into complete delirium, and she looked up to discover absolute horror contorting his cherubic features. He pointed behind her as shimmering tears began to stream down his face, mouth quivering in pure dread.

"Davey," she managed to blurt out. "Run… to the Warrens'."

He stood in shock, shaking his head in confusion. "Run! *Now!*"

The little boy darted off to the nearby house, and a sigh of relief escaped Shelley's lips as she saw a light go on inside. He would be safe; they had heard the screams… Now she just needed to save herself.

Crying out in agony, Shelley ran her hands down her right leg until her fingers felt something cold and thick lodged into the meat of her calf. Looking down, she realized it was a large, metal hook. A tortuous scream erupted, which throttled from her very core, and when the chain attached to the hook was yanked backward, her body was dragged along with it.

The world spun out of control now as she flailed along helplessly, pulled by an unknown force while her bare flesh brushed against the cool grass. She was being dragged to the large oak tree that stood at the corner of the property.

Once underneath the dark canopy of foliage, there was a brief reprieve as the chain fell to the ground in an abrasive metallic clatter. Then... silence. All Shelley could hear was her own breathing and the pounding of her terror-stricken heart. The pain in her calf had swelled to an almost numbing sensation.

Something gleamed above her now, reflected in the soft moonlight. As her eyes adjusted to the darkness, she saw the silhouette of a large figure, the figure she had just seen moments before. The gleam was coming from the object it held in its hand.

Placing her palms on the soft grass to push herself up, Shelley's eyes widened as her mind scrambled for the words to spare her life. The impact of the blade on her skull, however, rendered this useless.

As the blade sliced through fatty brain matter, severing blood vessels and nerves, Shelley's eyes fluttered shut.

1

SPOOK

Ghosts can't hurt you... ghosts can't hurt you... ghosts can't hurt you...

Abby repeated this phrase in her head as she sat on the living room floor of the old Victorian home. She was joined in a circle by her best friend, Val, and Val's two younger cousins, Jane and Bethany.

It was a fitting night for a séance. The storm clouds had just rolled in, and soft raindrops were beginning to pitter-patter against the stained-glass bay window.

Jane and Bethany were twins—both with straight, jet-black hair and bright blue eyes. Though just a few years younger, they were mature for their age... and very strange. The room was dark, save for the light of the three white pillar candles Jane and Bethany had bought for the occasion. Placed slightly outside of their circle on the oak wooden floor, the flames flickering atop each brought an air of foreboding.

The twins had grown up in this house, and Val had spent her childhood visiting them often. Though the three of them lauded how beautiful its decorative trim was and how the stained glass lent an authentic charm, Abby felt vulnerable within its mass of high ceilings and dark recesses.

The antique dolls situated throughout the house, heirlooms from the cousins' grandmother, did little to ease her concern. She'd seen enough horror movies about dolls coming to life and killing people to be terrified of them. Add the antique quality and that fear shot up a level. How someone could grow up in this house was beyond her; but what she saw as unpleasant, others saw as endearing.

Val had always had a penchant for the paranormal, and her cousins' interest in murder mysteries had helped fuel it. But a Ouija board seemed a bit much to Abby—almost child's play. Here they were, juniors in college. The whole charade felt ridiculous. But if the rumors that a woman named Holly Windsor had been murdered in this house in the late 1800s were true, then they just might be able to conjure up her spirit. At least Val and her cousins thought so.

As they held each other's hands, Abby shook her head.

"What?" Val asked, noticing her friend's unease.

"Just... this stuff creeps me out. You know that."

"Oh, c'mon. It's just good fun. Light as a feather, stiff as a board? Same thing."

"Doesn't seem like it to me. The candles and everything? This is a lot more than just faking levitation."

Abby had begrudgingly agreed to pick Val up tonight and drive her since Val's car was in the shop. Her cousins lived a half hour away, and with their parents being out for the night, it was the perfect opportunity. She'd done a lot of things for Val since they met back in middle school that she regretted. Spraying all of the cheerleaders' cars with shaving cream at after-school practice was just one of them. Sure, many of them were bitches, but Val had really twisted her arm on that one. Shaving cream left to dry in the sun destroys a paint job. Saint and sinner described their relationship perfectly.

Jane broke the silence, gesturing toward Val, who was leading this ceremony. "What next?"

"Well..." Val replied, looking at Abby. "For starters, *your* energy isn't helping that much."

"Are you *serious*?" Abby scoffed. "I drive you all the way here, and you want to *mock* me?"

Val shrugged. "Just sayin'. You're kinda killin' the vibe."

Abby sighed. "You *know* what I've fucking been through, right? You know what I saw. This shit's real, and… it's not a joke. I don't like playing around with this stuff."

"Listen. We *got* you. It's okay." Val squeezed Abby's hand gently and smiled. In turn, Abby managed to smile back, her eyes struggling to reciprocate.

"All I'm saying is… you open this door, you can't go back. Whatever you see will become a part of you. And some things aren't meant to be seen… some spirits are tortured souls," Abby said softly.

Jane and Bethany stared at Abby now, and she could detect slight mockery in their expressions. Here they were, younger than she was, with an exaggerated grit that gnawed at her very skin. They had no concept of the pure horror she'd witnessed; to them, this was just a silly game of dare.

Her mind now wandered to the ghost stories she'd heard as a kid, and the specific one that had always prickled her skin. It was the one about the woman in the woods. She couldn't quite remember where it had originated, but the legend had always spooked her: the spirit of a woman condemned to solitude, in an endless search for her children… the very children who had killed her and left her for dead.

She grew up near the woods as a kid and often had nightmares of waking up alone in the dark thicket in the midnight hour. A strange voice, the voice of a woman forlorn, would drift through the darkness.

She would look toward where the voice was coming from and see a woman floating to her horizontally with arms outstretched, clothed in a flowing white dress. The woman's mouth would open wide, and—

"Abby? Where'd you go?" Abby blinked her eyes and looked at Val, who was eyeing her with scrutiny.

"I... I'm fine. Let's just do this already."

Jane and Bethany smirked, and Abby sneered at them. Their expressions soon turned slack.

"Okay. Here we go." Val closed her eyes and breathed in deeply. Releasing her breath with a long exhale, she opened her eyes. "Holly Windsor. We call upon your spirit to join us."

They all waited in repose, hands clasped, as each of them glanced at each other in nervous anticipation. The storm outside had continued to brew, and soft lightning now illuminated the darkness of the expansive living room as the slow rumble of thunder followed. What had begun as scant rainfall outside had picked up, now an unsettling rhythm.

In the glow of lightning, Abby found herself staring at one of the dolls propped up against a throw pillow on the cream-colored sofa behind Jane and Bethany. It wore a dress with lace trim overlay, and a floral wreath adorned its head. Soft blonde curls framed a face that seemed to be staring at her right now. In the flashes of light, its eyes appeared to move, and every muscle in

Abby tensed as she fought the urge to flee right then and there. *Fuck antique dolls.*

After a few minutes of silence, Val spoke again. "Holly Windsor. Please join us in spirit." She considered her next words, then asked, "Are you with us?"

Again they sat, waiting for a sign. Anything. But there was nothing. As they remained silent, the lightning continued to flash in bursts as rumbling thunder followed.

"Can't that be a sign?" Jane asked. "The storm's stronger now."

"I don't think so," Val replied. As she opened her mouth to again invoke the spirit of Holly, a clash of thunder tore through the skies, seeming to rattle the very foundation of the Victorian home. They all jumped in fright, eyes wide with terror.

"W-was *that* a sign?" Bethany asked.

"Now I think we're getting somewhere," Val replied. "I think that was a sign. And she doesn't sound happy."

Rolling her eyes, Abby glanced down at her crossed legs, realizing she needed to shave again soon. Fresh stubble was beginning to appear. The drop of red liquid against her calf was unexpected, though. And when another warm drop splashed onto her bare skin, she lifted her gaze to see a pair of feet dangling between her and the twins. The skin was badly decomposed and even sloughed off in parts, revealing rotted tendons underneath.

Closing her eyes, Abby breathed in again, filling her lungs to capacity, then breathed out slow and steady. When she opened them, the rancid feet were still there. Blinking in response to a combination of absolute horror and utter paralysis, she leaned in and began to lift her gaze and follow sleek ankles that abruptly disappeared under a long, grainy skirt. The skirt ended at a svelte waist, which a soiled, tattered blouse was tucked into. Strands of black, matted hair lay against the sooty fabric, with some pieces almost weaving into the fibers. An oval face peered at Abby from within the thick, tangled mass of tresses, and black eyes curved upward as a smile spread across this woman's decrepit visage. *Holly.* The rope around her neck tightened, making her head quiver ever so slightly—and from the trail of blood running from the corner of her mouth, another drop spattered against Abby's forehead.

Screaming, Abby shot up and ran to the corner of the room, covering her eyes and sobbing hysterically.

"What the...?" Val ran to Abby's side, rubbing her arms and consoling her. *"Abby!"* she cried. "What the hell just happened?"

"I'm fucking *done*!" Abby spat at her friend. "No *more* of this!"

"Sweetie!" Val consoled her friend again.

"Don't *'sweetie'* me, Val!" Abby snarled. Looking to the middle of the room, she saw the twins now, sitting wide-eyed with a hint of wonder dancing across their faces. But the hanging lady had disappeared.

"Did you…" Val continued, cautiously. "Did you *see* something?"

Abby stared into Val's hopeful eyes and responded with a curt, "No." She wasn't about to play guinea pig for Val.

"Oh…" Val's voice trailed off. "Okay." She looked to her cousins, moving a finger across her neck in a sign that this séance was over, and Jane slouched and picked up the TV remote, flicking the screen to life.

"C'mon," Val said, placing her hands gently on Abby's shoulders. "Let's just… chill a bit, huh?"

Abby begrudgingly followed her friend back to the center of the room, sitting down and resting her back against the sofa like the others.

As Jane searched through the channels, Val leaned her head against Abby's shoulder. "Has Ben gotten back to you on that cabin yet?"

"No," Abby sighed, the tension in her melting now under Val's soft demeanor. "I mean, it'll be a miracle if he gets it. Sure would be nice, though."

After surfing through a few duds, Jane stopped on a rerun of a *Friday the 13th* movie. A cute blonde was trembling as Jason towered over her, ready to plunge a knife into her chest.

"Ooh!" Bethany chimed in, rubbing her hands together. "You guys ever hear about the babysitter murders? *You* know, the ones that happened in the early eighties. Some... what was it? Clatter, something, was his name? Found the babysitter, head was—"

Val rolled her eyes and looked at Bethany, shaking her head. "Let's just watch the movie."

Pursing her lips, Bethany looked to Jane and they both shrugged their shoulders, accepting their older cousin's orders.

"Your boyfriend's a turd if he doesn't get that cabin," Val whispered, nudging Abby with her shoulder.

Rolling her eyes, Abby couldn't help but agree somewhat with Val... though Ben was as sweet as could be. Summer break was already in full swing, and a carefree getaway with friends was definitely in order.

After a few seconds had passed, the twins eyed one another, then jumped up and ran to the kitchen. A few cupboards were opened, and the sound of kernels of corn popping in the microwave followed soon after. Excited giggles and the scuffing of bare feet on the floorboards signaled the twins' return, and the girls all bundled up together to indulge in the horror unfolding on the screen as the storm outside raged on.

While the oblivious campers were slaughtered one by one on the screen, Abby pondered the remoteness of the cabin Ben had been raving about.

2

BEGINNINGS

Abby had met Ben at a party two years ago, freshman year of college. She and Val had been lucky enough to dorm together that year, and Val, being the extrovert she was, had dragged Abby out. It was a fraternity party, something that made Abby want to gag. All these boys, testosterone leaking from their pores… just wasn't her thing. And she'd definitely been hit on by a bunch of brutes for the first hour or so. But then, out of the corner of her eye, she'd spotted a cute boy with blond curls chatting it up with a svelte brunette in the corner of the room. His gaze had averted to hers when he sensed her eyes on him, and she'd quickly looked away, feeling the hot blush rise in her cheeks. It was exacerbated by the third beer she had just downed. Unlike Val, she needed liquid courage.

Thinking it was just a gaze and nothing more, she'd wandered over to the kitchen, pushing through a mass of sweaty bodies to get a sip of water. Feeling the refreshing liquid coat her throat and cool her insides was divine. And as she closed her eyes and relished the brief moment before another beer fed her continuous dehydration, she heard a boy's voice. It was sweet with a bit of panache.

"Hitting it a bit hard tonight, huh? Slow down there, champ."

Opening her eyes, she saw the boy with blond curls standing next to her, leaning back casually against the wall with his arms crossed. His adorable mug was tilted, and curious blue eyes considered her current situation.

"Oh, I... thanks, but I'm okay." She realized there was a slight slur to her words but didn't care. "You can... you can go talk it up again with Little Miss Brunette."

"Ouch!" He put his hand to his heart. "Want to send me away that *soon*?"

Abby showcased her outfit with a gesture of her hand. "I'm literally wearing a hoodie, jeans, and sneakers. Miss Brunette's tits are practically popping out. And you want to stay here with *me*?" She rolled her eyes and stated rhetorically, *"Okay."*

"Miss *Brunette*, I must add, doesn't have much up *here*." He raised a hand and bopped his head with his pointer finger. Though Abby had her guard up, it certainly was beginning to crack.

They'd been inseparable for the rest of the party, and, even though Abby said she could walk herself back to her dorm (Val ended up not coming back until the morning), Ben had insisted he walk her back and won the argument.

After exchanging numbers, they'd realized they had a lot more in common than just people-watching drunk peers at parties. And he made her laugh. Boy, did he make her laugh! In addition to being smart and handsome, he was chivalrous too.

Loving him was easy, and it was fun. What she lacked, he made up for, and vice versa. Sure, they had their differences (he was more reserved than she was), but their relationship worked. It still bugged her from time to time that he could never understand what it was like to be the underdog, but she couldn't fault him for that. While Ben had practically been born popular, Abby spent many years in the lower ranks. It wasn't until college that she had a transformation, so to speak. She'd learned to appreciate her natural beauty and lean into her intuition. Learning to speak her mind had also given her more confidence, though Val still had a knack for short-circuiting that.

***

The trill of the phone on Abby's nightstand jarred her from her daydream down memory lane, and she jolted up. Since her mom didn't pick up after a few rings, she rolled her eyes and reached for the handset.

"Hello?" There was a croak in her voice, and she grimaced.

"Hey there, Kermit," Ben's voice sang from the other end of the line.

"You're a jerk! I'm still waking up, gimme a break."

"I won't give you a break, but I *will* give you some good news!"

"Is it... did you get the cabin?"

"I *did*! They had a last-minute cancellation, so get ready. Tomorrow we're off to cabin life."

"What? How did you *do* it? Isn't it, like, impossible to reserve?"

"Patience and persistence, babe. I've got lots of both."

"Well, I guess you *do*." Then she thought of the rooms. "Wait. How many rooms? And couples only, right?"

"No, Dustin's going too."

"Really?"

"Yeah. What do you got against Dustin? You're always weird about him."

"Nothing! I just... didn't know he was going."

Dustin was one of Ben's best friends and was really a big teddy bear. He'd hit on Abby before she'd met Ben, and she'd turned him down, oblivious at the time that he was good friends with Ben. Though he was adorable, he just wasn't her type. Being chill was a good thing, but he was a bit *too* carefree—and a bit scruffy. She never wanted to cause any rift between Ben and Dustin; even if she *did* say something, it would surely blow over, but she was playing it safe. It was obvious that Dustin was, too. He'd become quieter when around her and Ben.

"Okay... we're all gonna get along, *right*?" Ben quipped on the other end of the line.

"Of *course* we are! Jesus, Ben. I'm not a kid."

"I know, I know... Well, hey, we're staying for four nights, long weekend. Dustin's gonna meet us there. You okay driving? My dad's car broke down, so he needs to use mine for the weekend."

"What is it with all these *cars* breaking down?"

"What do you mean?"

"Oh, just... I drove Val out to her cousin's house last night. Her car's in the shop, too."

"Who the hell knows. I gotta bounce, though. Check-in's at three, takes about three hours to get there. Leave around twelve tomorrow?"

"Sounds great! And thanks, Ben, really. This is gonna be awesome. Hey—we get dibs on the biggest room, right? Since you booked this place?"

"Hell *yeah*, we do! Master bedroom is huge. Big-ass bed, too, if you know what I mean."

Abby felt tingles down below and bit her lower lip just thinking about Ben's large hands wandering over her soft skin. "Well, that just means you and I will have to break it in... for the umpteenth time." She could sense his boyish grin on the other end of the line.

"Damn, girl. You got me all excited now... Shit." She smiled, twirling the phone cord in her fingers. "Okay," Ben said after a titillating pause. "See you tomorrow. Love you."

"Love you, too."

Abby hung up, then fell back onto the bed and looked to the ceiling, smiling. This weekend was going to be epic. Good friends, a lakeside cabin, and the getaway they all needed together. A hint of sadness crept in, though, as she thought of senior year approaching.

Change was scary, but they all had each other. Nothing could ever tear them apart.

3

A WARM DEPARTURE

Abby's mom was in the living room, drinking her morning coffee and reading the newspaper, when Abby headed downstairs and passed by to the kitchen. She needed to pack her favorite coffee mug. It had been a gift from her dad, and was embellished with the words, "Favorite Daughter". She had no siblings, so it had been an inside joke.

"You sure you have everything?" her mom called out.

"I do, Mom. It's only a few days."

"Oh my *God*!" her mom cried from the other room.

"What?"

"Have you *heard* about this? Some cannibal death cult they discovered out in the desert? What the hell is the world *coming* to?"

Abby shook her head as a nervous laugh escaped her lips. "Well, at least I'm just going to PA."

Her mom stood up, shaking her head in disbelief, then placed her palms on Abby's cheeks. "Thank *God*! You just be careful, okay?"

"Mom, I'll be *fine*."

With a huff, Abby picked up her duffel bag.

"Okay. Well, have fun! And remember, call if you need anything."

"I will. Love you." Giving her mom a hug and a kiss on the cheek, Abby then bounced out the front door with zest; she was eager to see Ben, wrap her arms around him, and plant her lips on his.

As she stepped outside, luxurious sunshine warmed her ivory skin. It was early June, and the weather was perfect—delightfully warm with not a cloud overhead. Placing her duffel bag in the trunk of her Jeep Grand Cherokee, she started the engine and headed out. Checking the clock, she was doing good on time. It was only 11 a.m., and she had to pick up Val and Jamie after Ben.

Jamie was Val's new boyfriend, and also Ben's best friend. Though Ben had met Dustin in college, he'd known Jamie since middle school. He wasn't a fan of his best friend dating *Val*, but he rolled with it. She'd dug her claws into Jamie a few months ago, and it seemed he was enjoying the wild ride. As opposed to Val's intense nature, Jamie was much more chill: opposites attract.

They were lucky—aside from Dustin, everyone lived within a half hour of each other. As she drove on, Abby turned on the radio, anticipating which song would burst into the quiet of the cabin. "All I Wanna Do" by Sheryl Crow danced in her ears, and she bopped her head, singing along to the catchy tune. It was a sign... a sign this weekend was going to be a damn good one.

Ben was sitting on the front steps when she pulled up to his house. One look at her and he sported a wild grin, throwing his arms up in excitement. With a girlish giggle, she opened the door and ran to him. Wrapping his arms around her, he lifted her up, and she clasped his face in her hands, kissing him with every fiber of her being. As he lowered her gently to the ground, they gazed into each other's eyes.

"Oh, babe. I can't *wait*!" Abby cried.

"I know. Still can't believe we got the place."

"Well, tell me how much it was. We'll all pitch in, pay you our shares."

He looked back at his house. "My mom and dad said they'd pay for the whole thing... an early birthday present."

"What? I know your parents have money, but that's *crazy*!"

"They got a deal. You know how my dad is."

Abby wrinkled her nose.

"Okay, okay... we get back, we can figure something out," Ben said. "But *now*..." He raised his arms up again, eyes wide, "...let's *do* this already! I wanna get the hell *outta* here!"

With a devilish grin, Abby kicked her leg up and popped open the trunk of the Jeep for Ben. After throwing his bag in, Abby asked if he could drive the first leg of the trip.

"Sure. Off to Val's now?" Ben asked.

"Yeah, Jamie's there with her."

Rolling his eyes and smiling, Ben put the Jeep in drive and they headed off. He knew Abby and Val were a packaged deal.

4

CHILL

Abby lifted her face to the sky and closed her eyes, basking in the luxurious summer rays pouring in through the open moonroof as the Jeep sped along. The miniature dreamcatcher charm her mom had bought her for her birthday two years ago hung on the rearview mirror, its purple feathers dancing in the breeze. A dreamcatcher hung on the wall above the railing of her bed frame at home, too, ever since she was a kid. It was her dad's way of making her feel safe when she had suffered a bout of nightmares around six years old. The charm took her back to that time and made her feel her dad was always with her. He'd died from a heart attack when she was just eleven. Carefree was a feeling she yearned to still possess in spades, but much of it had left when he left her. He had been the embodiment of carefree.

Looking to her left, Abby smiled at Ben. He smiled back with that adorable grin she'd been smitten with the first time they'd met. He was even wearing the same college cap he'd worn that night—on backward as always, showcasing adorable blond curls that brushed his tan skin. He lifted his right hand from the steering wheel and pinched her chin, a gesture that always sent her heart fluttering. The feeling of freedom rushing to the surface now was exhilarating. No more studying, no more essay writing, and no more grade anxiety. Just sweet sunshine, good friends, and cold beer.

Val hadn't been ready when they had picked them up, and Abby wasn't surprised. Jamie had just shrugged his shoulders as Val ran back into the house for the fourth time to make sure she had everything she needed. Abby reminded her there would be several opportunities to buy anything she may have forgotten on the way there (well, almost anything), but her words had dispersed into the wind. When Val was finally ready, they had all froze, waiting for her to run back inside. But there was no more crying wolf, and they'd finally been able to set off.

Jamie and Val were now in the back seat, and Dustin would be meeting them at the cabin. And the beer? There were plenty of six-packs already in the trunk that they'd stopped to pick up, while Dustin had the rest covered. The clinking of glass bottles in the back signaled the dulling of senses and sweet relaxation awaiting to be partaken when they arrived.

They were off to Reeves Cabin. Ben had been hearing rumblings about it on campus since the end of last year. Located in northern Pennsylvania, it was notoriously difficult to rent. Most summers, you'd find yourself out of luck. Ben had really been tenacious, though. The last-minute opportunity seemed serendipitous with next year being their senior year—graduation loomed with a sense of uncertainty, and these two years together in college had been so memorable. What better way to kick off this summer, though. The cabin boasted a beautiful lakeside view, a jacuzzi, a decked-out entertainment room, and an expansive master bedroom on the third floor that Abby and Ben had already claimed.

The location of the cabin was what set it apart from the rest. Nestled in the backcountry of Pennsylvania, the view was supposed to be spectacular. Though Abby was excited to have the privacy, the thought of isolation had crept in from time to time. In a different state, in a cabin, in the middle of nowhere. Ben caught the slight unease in her expression from the corner of his eye.

"You okay?"

"Oh yeah, I'm fine," she replied, sporting a cheery smile.

Looking out the window, Abby noticed how stark the scenery had become. Visions of that night began to play over in her mind again. She cringed, trying to divert her thoughts. Regina haunted her still, and it was a horrifying memory she alone carried.

5

ABBY'S DARKNESS

Abby had seen a ghost before the séance, though it wasn't something she particularly liked to talk about. The thought of it brought her back to 3 a.m. on that balmy Saturday morning in early May just two years ago. Everyone says 3 a.m. is the witching hour: turns out they're right.

She'd only known Regina since the past September, when they were paired together freshman year as college roommates. Regina was an interesting one. Full of zest and vigor, but also sharp as a knife when she needed to be. Abby never let on how much she was intimidated by her roommate, but she assumed her body language conveyed it quite clearly. Whenever Regina would burst into the room, Abby would shy away and coil up, wanting nothing more than to block that erratic energy.

Regina had a soft side as well, though. On lazy afternoons, sometimes they would both sit on the bed together—she'd brush and braid Abby's hair and tell her all about her wildest escapades. Abby would listen contentedly, musing over how invigorating it must have felt to crash exquisite parties and how courageous it was to hitchhike state to state in search of adventure and discovery. Their lives couldn't have been more different, but Abby did find comfort in her roommate's savviness and street smarts. What Regina lacked that Abby had in spades, though, was intuition. And that's what led to her roommate's untimely death.

Friday evening started out as most other Friday evenings had recently for Regina; she headed out to meet her new boyfriend of two months and get into who knew what manner of hijinks together. Abby didn't like him, but her taste in men was quite different. While she sought out intelligence and humor, Regina sought out mischief and cunning—and her boyfriend Devon possessed an abundance of these qualities. Though Abby wasn't one to judge others on appearances, she had no problem judging him. Whenever he'd meet Regina at the dorm, he'd eye Abby with an air of superiority; sometimes it even seemed he was mentally undressing her. Gross was the best way to explain it—yet whenever she voiced this to Regina, it fell on deaf ears.

Regina was murdered that night, and it sent the entire college community into a frenzy of terror. Abby discovered her lifeless body the next day after returning from a one-night camping trip with friends—she was arranged in such a peculiar manner on the bed, with her arms and legs softly crossed as if in sweet repose. Her hands gently rested on a svelte stomach that had been stabbed multiple times, and her eyelids had been pushed down to cover those fiery green eyes.

The harrowing scream that tore from Abby's throat upon finding Regina had been a warning alarm, and it was hard to remember much of what happened next. She could still feel the embraces of her dorm peers; palms ran gentle circles across her back seeking to comfort and protect. Soft, heartfelt murmurs danced to her ears. And all the while, Abby fixated on the slack body on her bed, not able to look away. Shock had prevented her from being able to move. All she could do was gawk and contemplate who that person was. Of course it was Regina, but it was too horrifying to believe.

No one had any doubts as to who the murderer was, and weeks later, her boyfriend was charged with her death. As it turned out, he'd been tied to another murder that had occurred in the area a year prior.

Family support was crucial during the weeks after Regina's death. Abby moved back home in the aftermath, needing the space to process and recover. Her mom blanketed her with love, and many nights were spent sobbing in the warmth of her embrace. She'd never witnessed such cold, ruthless horror firsthand.

In time, Abby eventually found her footing again in her new dorm room. Her new roommate, Val, was a bit eccentric, but her quirky sarcasm softened Abby's lingering frayed edges.

Abby had declined Val's invitation to attend a fraternity party that particular Friday night in May, exactly a month after Regina's murder. In hindsight, she should have gone. It would have saved her another horrifying experience—this one much more traumatizing than discovering Regina in the dorm room weeks ago. It had been a long day, though, and the idea of attempting to mingle with a bunch of horny guys sounded like torture.

When Val had closed the door behind her as she headed out, and silence had finally fallen upon the room, Abby was able to let out a long, slow breath and revel in her solitude. While time alone was unnerving to some, she found it a way to recharge. No outside noise, no distractions... just you and your thoughts.

Falling asleep had been easy, and she'd kept the blinds open so the luminous full moon could lull her to slumber. And slumber she did... until a sound woke her up. It was a punchy, wet sound. Chalking it up to another episode of sleep paralysis (she'd had many recently), she readied herself to work through this bout of wakeful REM. But she had been able to wince, and she was able to wiggle her fingers and toes too. This wasn't sleep paralysis, and she wasn't alone. Then came the sound again—it resonated from Val's bed on the other side of the room near the window. She'd probably brought a guy back from the party. That didn't sound like fucking, though.

Sitting up, she rubbed her eyes and looked over to Val's bed. There, sitting on her new roommate's bed with eyes fixated on her, was Regina. She was wearing the same white crop top she'd been wearing the night of her murder, and her hand was moving back and forth rhythmically in front of her stomach. Trails of tears glimmered on her cheeks in the soft moonlight, and something else gleamed in her hand. It was a kitchen knife, and she was methodically stabbing herself in the stomach.

Abby's jaw clamped tight, and her eyes widened in fear. Now it really did feel as if she had succumbed to sleep paralysis, yet this was very real. She wanted to bolt out of bed and sprint out the door, but feared what Regina's reaction would be. So there she sat, panicked eyes locked with the sullen ones of her murdered roommate.

Then Regina uttered something under her breath... something Abby couldn't discern. And as Regina uttered this unintelligible phrase, her brow furrowed and her mouth twisted, hot and spiteful. The next time she whispered this phrase, Abby could understand.

"I didn't listen."

Regina's lament rose from a soft whisper to a normal tone. But then she began to stab herself faster, and her face became morose as anguish twisted her features. What had been a normal tone now erupted into a pestilent shriek.

"I DIDN'T LISTEN! I DIDN'T LISTEN! I DIDN'T—"

Abby sprang from the bed and sprinted out the door, and the rest was a haze. Eventually, she had found herself in another dorm room, being comforted by complete strangers. Yet it had taken some time for the fear to dissipate into sorrow.

Some said she was one of the *lucky* ones. What was that term? Ah, yes—a clairvoyant, able to connect with the spiritual realm. But what weight she had to carry because of this ability could never be understood by others, and it made anything involving the paranormal utterly terrifying.

6

LET'S GET LIT

There was silence as the Jeep rambled on, rougher now with the paved roads becoming uneven. Ben placed his hand on Abby's thigh, and she looked toward him, forcing a curt smile as the image of Regina's tormented spirit finally vanished from her thoughts. Though the memory was sure to return again, Abby hoped she'd have a longer respite this time.

"When we gonna get there?" Val's shrill voice cut through the silence, and Ben cringed. Nails on a chalkboard was the best way to describe it, God bless her.

Abby turned her head to face Val, who sat diagonal to her in the back seat, and chuckled. "Patient much?"

Val rolled her head, then let it fall back against the headrest. "It's just... I need to go pee. Like... really bad."

"We're almost there," Ben replied. "Only fifteen minutes. I see Lakeside Drive up ahead."

Abby lifted her sunglasses to rest them on her head and turned back to Val. "Can you hold it? We're *so* close!"

Grimacing, Val placed her hands between her legs and shook her thighs back and forth. "I think I can. I mean... if I can't, you're gonna have some cleanup to do back here, Ben."

"Maybe I can make you feel better, babe." Jamie placed his hand on Val's knee and caressed the length of her bare thigh to her crotch.

"Jamie, you touch her right now, and I swear I'll punch you in the fucking *dick*!" Val screamed.

Ben shook his head, chuckling. Eyeing Jamie from the rearview mirror, Ben watched his friend wincing now, hands held up in surrender. Jamie was an odd one. He was sweet as could be, but not too bright when it came to girls. How he and Val had hooked up was still a mystery, but it didn't hurt that he gave in to her every demand. Not the *healthiest* relationship, but it worked for now.

Their backgrounds couldn't have been more different—Val's parents had divorced when she was just eight years old, and she had grown up after that with little parental supervision. They just couldn't be bothered by her, it seemed. Jamie, on the other hand, had been raised in a religious household where he had loving (sometimes overbearing) parents. He'd never admitted it, but it was obvious he yearned for spontaneity and mischief, something Val had in copious amounts. It always was good fun when she could break his hard candy shell. Though he was reserved with strangers and presented to the world as serious and careful, she brought out the little kid in him. Abby saw it as adorable, and Ben saw it as annoying. Whatever the case, their relationship was here to stay.

The landscape had turned even more stark now, and bare fields whooshed by as they drove on. Farms dotted the countryside, and cows could be seen contentedly nibbling on grass.

One building farther down was particularly larger than the rest and loomed menacing amidst the tranquil farms. It was situated on a sprawling plot of land near the stop sign they were approaching, with multiple dark windows in varying sizes running the length of the weathered stone facade.

"Uh, yeah. That's a bit creepy," Ben uttered.

"Ooh!" Val shrieked, so shrill that Jamie covered his ears. "Guys, look! Look at the piggies! Oh, they're so *cute*!"

A few pigs could be seen from the road, huddled in a tight group.

"Eww," Jamie scoffed. "No thanks, pigs are disgusting—and they reek, too."

"One, pigs are not disgusting. They're actually very clean," Abby retorted. "And two, they're super smart. People give 'em a bad rap."

"Abby's right," Val chimed in. "Probably smarter than you!" she scoffed, jabbing Jamie in the side.

Jamie just shook his head and rolled his eyes. "The shit I deal with, I swear…"

Abby snickered, then looked at the building now as they pulled to a stop. It leered back at her in morbid silence, seeming to hold a dark secret. Nothing good happened within its stony confines—quite the opposite. "Guys, this isn't just some building. It looks like… I don't know. Some kind of *prison* or something. No good vibes in that place."

"You guys up for some bacon?" Ben laughed, eyeing the pigs.

"Um, *no* thanks," Abby snapped back. "Place gives me the creeps. Just, let's go already."

As the Jeep drove on, the building became smaller in the side view mirror, and Abby was thankful when it eventually disappeared from sight.

Val's voice cut through the stillness. "You said we're almost there, Ben! I don't see *anything*. Just fields!"

"My Garmin says it's only ten minutes away now," Ben replied, rolling his eyes at Abby. She smiled and shook her head.

"I saw that, Abby! Is Ben up to his old shit again? You know you're stuck with me, right, Ben?"

"No, no..." Ben chimed from the front seat. "You're lovely to be around, Val. Just *lovely*!"

"Asshole," Val mumbled and kneed the back of Ben's seat. This was met with uproarious laughter, to which she kneed it again.

"You guys, c'mon. You're like brother and sister, I *swear*!" Abby laughed.

"Oh, damn! There it is!" Jamie pointed off to the right.

Torn from their playful chatter, the rest of them looked to the right as well. The sign for Lakeside Drive was in clear view, and beyond it, atop a hill in the distance, sat a stunning A-frame. An expansive forest sprawled out on each side of the cabin, framing it within a sea of trees. Abby's heart picked up a bit, but after a few deep breaths, it settled. She wasn't expecting the location to be so secluded.

"Wow. We're really in the middle of nowhere, aren't we?" Val said. Then she grinned at Jamie and stroked his thigh. "What happens in the woods stays in the woods."

"What happens between you both stays far away from *me*!" Ben called out from the driver's seat. Looking in the rearview mirror, he spied Val devouring Jamie in a sloppy kiss and stuck out his tongue in disgust.

As Ben turned right onto Lakeside Drive, the beautiful lake came into view on the left. A soft breeze caressed the surface, creating an endless procession of shimmering ripples. Reeves Cabin was visible on the other side—its large window visage stood elegant against the summer foliage.

"It's even more beautiful than the pictures you showed me," Abby gasped, looking at Ben.

He nodded, pursing his lips. "Sure is. You know what's more beautiful, though? You in that blue bikini."

Abby bit her lower lip and chuckled, tilting her head and raising her pinkie to her lips.

"Gross," Val scoffed from the back seat.

"Like you guys *aren't*?" Abby fired back.

"No! We're really *not*." Val tickled Jamie's ear with her fingers. "Because *Jamie* here won't play the games *I* wanna play."

"Okay, you can stop it right there, Val. I don't want to hear about your *games*." Ben cringed and shook his head in disgust.

"Oh, you'll be *hearing* them! Maybe tonight. That okay with you?"

"*Eww!*" Abby laughed. "Val, how did your *games* suddenly become the topic of discussion? We're nipping this, right now!" She ran her palm horizontally along the front of her neck, pronouncing the topic dead. The rope tightening around Holly Windsor's throat flashed before Abby's eyes as she made that hand gesture, and visions of the specter's rancid features sent a flurry of shivers up her spine. So much for keeping those thoughts at bay.

They were driving along the far edge of the lake now, curving around to the opposite side. Though the cabin sat alone in the distance, they had passed many houses before the bend. Normal-looking houses, which at least offered a feeling of safety. They hadn't crossed over into strange country. The massive lake magnified their sheer distance from Reeves Cabin, however. As they rounded the bend, Ben could already see the gleam of Dustin's black Chevy in the driveway. "How'd he *beat* us here?"

"Because he's got an Impala *SS*, dude." Jamie laughed from the back seat. "He can run circles around this thing."

"Yeah, yeah..." Ben shrugged off Jamie's snark.

As they pulled up alongside Dustin, a billow of smoke wafted from the driver's side door, carrying the sweet, pungent smell of weed with it. Dustin smiled wide from the driver's seat, squinting his eyes as he took another drag of his joint. He was the bona fide joker of the group and lived life in slow motion.

"I hope he's got enough of that for all of us," Abby muttered.

"*Oh*, yeah. Dustin never disappoints," Ben quipped as he shifted her Jeep into park.

Dustin opened the door and stepped out, handing the joint to Abby. "I *heard* you." Then he bowed in a curtsy. "Enjoy, m'lady. There's lots more where that came from."

Abby smiled and snickered back. "Good." After taking a long drag, she lifted her gaze to the sky, a wispy cloud of smoke rising from her puckered lips.

"Y-eah!" Dustin grinned and nodded.

Passing the joint around, each of them succumbed to sweet relaxation, and the mood was set. The stunning A-frame beckoned them to enter. A visage of windows, it offered a gorgeous view of the lake—and an uninhibited view inside.

7

REEVES CABIN

A spacious, rustic interior greeted them upon opening the front door. Off to the right of the living room sat a tan leather sectional, with a decorative rouge rug. To the front of it stood a beautiful wooden table, its knots whirling along the smooth, polished surface. On the left side of the living room, across from the sectional, sat a matching loveseat, next to which there was a leather mocha-colored recliner.

Dustin threw his duffel bag on the floor and plopped in the recliner, lifting the recline and sporting a thumbs-up. Jamie sat on the loveseat and discovered it had recliners as well, which took Dustin down a notch. As Ben sat down on the sectional to join his friends, Abby and Val continued a self-guided tour, marveling at their home for the next few days.

A modest kitchen beamed from behind the living room. Cream-colored granite countertops graced the waist-high cabinets along the wall, across from which there sat a long island spanning the length of the cabinets. The same striking granite countertop lined the top of the island, and five chairs sat flush along the outer edge.

"Ben—always down to a T," Val commented, referencing the perfect number of chairs.

"That he is!" Abby chimed, her tone a bit sarcastic.

"What?" Val asked, confused.

"Oh, it's just… sometimes I feel like…" Abby's voice trailed off. "*I don't know. Just like I'm along for the ride.*"

"What does *that* mean?"

"Well… He's perfect, I'm not." She looked to the floor. "I dunno. I know it's stupid, me thinking this way."

"Little bit!" Val responded, tilting her head and accentuating this thought with her pointer finger touching her thumb. "Listen, you're not that super shy girl anymore. Stop thinking that way. Besides, you got that killer bod. *Own* that shit."

Abby smirked and shot Val a sly smile. "I do, don't I?"

Val smiled sweetly, rolling her eyes. "*Yes*. Legs for days, that tight ass, and those perky tits. Now onward, I'm done doling out compliments."

Shaking her head, Abby chuckled. "Hit your limit, huh?"

Pursing her lips, Val tilted her head. "Soak it in."

In an effort to nip this conversation, they both looked toward the front of the house again, their eyes spanning the distressed wooden dining room table. Circular in shape, thin streaks of varying colors ran its width, ranging from light tan to dark caramel. Abby ran her fingers along the smooth surface as they both pulled out a chair and sat down, marveling at the lakeside view. "This view... and this house! It's *gorgeous*."

"Yeah, it really is," Val replied, leaning back in her chair. "Expensive as all *hell,* though. I can't believe Ben's parents bought this for us."

"Ben said they got a deal on this, but... sometimes I think he just wants me to feel less guilty, because he knows my mind goes there. They've always been that way, though—pitching in." Abby hunched over and cringed. "Like that trip I went on last year with Ben's family? To the Caribbean? Ben's parents paid for the *whole* trip—airfare and everything."

Val shrugged her shoulders, smirking. "I mean, you got a free trip to the freakin' *Caribbean*. Like... don't feel bad about that. If you don't want to go next time"—she nudged Abby's shoulder—"I'll happily take your place. Just... poor Ben'll be left high and dry."

Abby rolled her eyes and shook her head. "You never cease to amaze me."

Val nuzzled into the crook of Abby's neck. "You know you *love* me, though!"

Grimacing, Abby looked over to the boys, and Val followed her gaze. Ben, Jamie, and Dustin were talking about the countless parties at Dustin's place last summer. Since Dustin's parents were hardly ever home, his house was the party house. It was just too bad he lived so much farther away than the rest of them. Didn't stop them from all crashing over at his place, though. When his parents did make rare appearances, they were never bothered by the cloud of pot smoke billowing up from the finished basement they all kicked back in. And while his dad was a man of few words, his mom was all smiles and sunshine.

As the boys continued to banter, Ben launched a throw pillow at Dustin, which he launched right back at Ben's face. Standing up, Ben shook his head and sneered, then dove down and hooked Dustin in a mean headlock.

"Dude!" Dustin cried out between fits of laughter. "You threw it first! What the *hell*, man?"

"Say *uncle*!" Ben laughed as he ground a noogie on Dustin's head.

Jamie fell back against the loveseat, clapped his hands, and roared with laughter.

As this ruckus continued, Abby and Val looked at each other and shook their heads in bewilderment.

Squinting at the boys and placing her elbow on the table, Val rested her chin in her palm and cocked her head. "They really don't ever grow up, do they? Still little boys."

Laughing, Abby crossed her arms and leaned back in her chair. "No, they don't."

After finally letting go of poor Dustin, Ben stood up and clapped his hands, demanding everyone's attention. "Okay. Who's up for a swim?"

"Now?" Abby exclaimed. "We just got here. Just want to chill for a bit."

"Well if *you* aren't joining me," Ben quipped, pointing at Val, "maybe *Val* will." He took off his shirt to reveal his taut chest, and Val swooned. "Oh, I'm *comin'*, baby!" After slamming her hand on the table, she giggled and ran to join Ben as he opened the sliding door to the front deck.

"Val—you don't even have your *swimsuit* on," Abby called as her friend stepped out.

Removing her gray T-shirt and jean shorts, Val now stood before them wearing just black lace panties and a bra. She loosened her ebony hair from her ponytail, and it fell in loose waves against her light brown skin. "Who says you need one?" Then she winked at Jamie, whose tongue was practically dragging on the ground. "You comin'?"

"Uh, y-yeah," he managed to stutter.

"Go get your *girl*, man!" Dustin laughed. "Or else Ben will!"

Abby rolled her eyes at Dustin as she stood up.

"What?" He smirked.

"*You* know what!" Hurling a throw pillow at him, she smiled and headed to her duffel bag to grab her swimsuit.

Everyone was in the lake when Abby walked out onto the dock. She had one of those CoverGirl moments where the breeze swept her light brown hair just right, and the afternoon sun felt glorious on her skin. Everyone else was frolicking except for Ben—he was treading in place, staring at her with a cheeky grin.

"Hey, beautiful. Come in already!"

Lowering her head with a mischievous smirk, Abby took a few steps back. Then with a running start, she cannonballed into the water, sending everyone reeling. A splash fest ensued, and laughter filled the air. They were all kids again, with not a care in the world.

It was one of those precious moments you remember your whole life... a moment they reveled in until hunger called and the faint full moon beckoned nightfall.

8

TO FRIENDSHIP

As the sun began to turn blood orange against the western horizon, everyone sat lounging on the deck sipping chilled beers. Everyone except for Ben, who was preheating the grill—a plate of juicy ground beef patties awaited his signature flair. He never gave his secret away, and not even Abby knew the recipe for his seasoning. As he sprinkled the savory blend of ingredients on the raw patties, Dustin approached and hovered over his shoulder.

"You'll never find out, you know." Ben laughed without looking over his shoulder. "So don't even try. Never giving my holy grail away. Go—sit! Stop fucking breathing on me, man." He playfully jabbed Dustin in the stomach with his elbow, and Dustin held his hands up in surrender. He turned around and walked over to the others who were seated on the cushioned wicker chairs surrounding the glass-covered deck table.

"I tried... but I failed." Drooping his head down, he plopped down next to Jamie.

"Chillax," Val said with ease. "We ain't never getting that recipe, and you know it. But even if you had it, you don't know how to grill!" She gestured toward Ben. "Leave it to the master."

"*Ouch*, Val." Sitting stoically with his gaze to the sky, Dustin proclaimed, "A man can learn."

"A man can also just sit his ass down and enjoy a cold one."

Dustin bowed his head and clicked bottles with Val. "Touché, my friend."

The sizzle of raw meat snapped in the air as Ben placed the patties on the grill. A warm breeze followed shortly after, carrying with it the seductive aroma of summer barbecue. It ruffled the leaves of the trees and lightly brushed their damp swimsuits draped over the railing. Jamie wrapped his arm around Val, and she leaned her head on his shoulder. Everything was perfect, and their world felt... complete.

Abby raised her bottle to the others in a toast. "To friendship."

"To friendship," they all reciprocated with the clinking of bottles.

"Ben, get over here!" Abby called over her shoulder with her bottle held high.

He grabbed the beer he was milking on the table next to the grill and came over to complete the toast. "Burgers are ready, guys. You all hungry?"

"Famished!" Dustin leaned back and placed the back of his palm to his forehead, exposing a flash of potbelly underneath his Hawaiian shirt.

"Pfft, famished..." Abby gibed, slapping his gut.

"Easy," he said, rubbing his belly. "I'll have you know, the ladies love this." He gestured to Ben, who now sauntered over with the burgers. "Besides, we can't all look like *Ken* over here."

"Ken doesn't have curls," Abby quipped, beaming at Ben.

"Well, Ben... Ken. I mean..." Dustin shrugged. "I'm not *wrong*."

Ben waved them off with a flick of his hand. "What you guys should *really* be talking about right now is these *burgers*. Dig in!"

"Yes, *please*," Jamie replied. "Thanks, man." He fist-bumped Ben.

"Yeah, thanks Ben," Val replied. "Sorry we're all a bunch of losers when it comes to cooking."

"Nah, it's all good. But *breakfast* tomorrow"—he pointed to Jamie—"is on *this* guy."

"Yum." Val crossed her arms, grabbing her knees and lovingly nudging Jamie.

Jamie nodded and pointed back at Ben. "This is the burger guy, but I'm the *breakfast* guy."

Dustin raised his hands. "If you say so. Oh, and... I like my eggs sunny side up, with just a *dash* of salt and pepper."

"You'll get your eggs scrambled, just like everyone else."

"Well, it was worth a try."

After laughing off Dustin's failed attempt, they all dug in, relishing their first dinner together at Reeves Cabin. The sun was setting on the horizon now, casting everything in beautiful ruby gold hues. With the wind having died down, the lake behind them stood still, a glassy reflection of the windswept oranges and yellows above. Nighttime was calling, with a sense of mischief.

9

Campfire Stories

Ben tended to the fire pit, adding in another piece of firewood to keep it going strong. The pit had been a pile of burnt embers before, but thankfully they'd found a hefty stack of firewood on the side of the house. Everyone sat around, mesmerized by the writhing, crackling flames. There's something about an open flame under bright moonlight that conjures up mystery and intrigue, and they'd found themselves sharing ghost stories and urban legends.

When Jamie had offered to tell one, he talked about the infamous house at the end of his street. Last one on the left, as it turned out.

"You've never been *in* that house, though—right?" Val asked Jamie. "But it's at the end of your street, so... I mean, *I* would have gone in."

"*Hell* no! There's always been stories, though... ever since I was a kid. About what happened before we were born. My brother said he went in there once—I was about eight, I think, so he was twelve. Broke in with one of his friends. Said they saw some kind of *aura* in the kitchen. You know, like, some floating light."

"Maybe the ghost was gonna make some *tacos*," Dustin jeered as he took a drag of his joint and passed it to Ben.

Jamie shook his head and rolled his eyes. "*Seriously*, dude? Like... how are you even here? How do you even operate? You're always fuckin' high as a kite."

"*Ouch*, babe. That's harsh," Val said.

"Straight A's almost all year, motherfucker," Dustin snapped back. "I can still operate just fine because, news flash"—he held his hands up, mimicking jazz hands—"I'm not always high as a kite. So mind your own damn business."

Jamie rolled his eyes as he shook his head, then heaved his shoulders and sighed. "Anyway, the family was murdered. Like... the whole family. Kids and everything. I don't think they'd be making *tacos*."

"Just sayin'. Tacos are good, man."

"Whatever... Gimme that." Ben passed the joint to Jamie, who saw Dustin side-eye him but paid it no mind.

"You're all sittin' here talkin' 'bout doors creaking open by themselves, *eerie* lights floating around, scratching sounds in the attic—probably just squirrels, by the way—but have you ever heard of the Clatter Man?"

"The *Clatter* Man?" Abby asked. "Um, *no*. Is that, like, some messed-up doll or something? Like Chucky? You wind it up and it doesn't *murder* you, but—just follows you around with some cymbals?" She laughed so hard at the absurdity she snorted.

"Oh, you guys haven't *heard* of him," Dustin said, eyes wide.

"No," Ben replied. "We haven't heard of the *Clatter* Man. I mean, if he's supposed to be scary... sure don't *sound* like it."

"Oh, he's *scary* all right. You guys never heard of the babysitter murders? Word is the babysitter's boyfriend conjured him up. He got sliced, and she got hooked. They found her the next day and her head was split open. Kid she was babysitting was fine, though. So was the family dog."

"Oh, the *doggie*! Thank goodness!" Val chirped.

"*Seriously*, Val? What about the kid?" Abby retorted.

"Well, yeah—that too." Val shrugged.

"Don't like this, don't wanna hear any more," Abby told Dustin. "Screw this *conjuring* shit."

Dustin waved her off with his hand. "Oh, c'mon. It's just urban legend. *But*... if you guys want to hear a *real* scary story, I got one."

As they all fell quiet, a silent deliberation floating among them, it began to drizzle.

"Are you serious?" Ben moaned.

"It's just a drizzle," Abby replied. "No biggie."

"Yeah, but a drizzle can lead to—" It began to pour.

"Let's bounce!" Jamie exclaimed as they all ran back in, Abby and Val giggling with childish glee.

After they had changed into dry clothes and fetched some more beer, they found themselves lounging in the living room staring at Dustin, who was the last to grab a bottle from the fridge. He sensed eyes on him and looked their way.

"What?"

"*You* know what!" Val replied.

He pursed his lips, eyes wide, and shrugged.

"The *Clatter* Man, Dustin!" Val brushed her hair back and leaned against Jamie's chest as they sat on the sectional. She crossed one leg over the other, her foot rocking casually.

"I still don't like this," Abby muttered.

"C'mon, Abby. It's just an urban legend. Like that guy with a hook," Ben replied. "You never hear of couples getting attacked in the park by some hook-wielding *lunatic*. It's just to scare you... stupid fun."

Abby scooted herself toward the edge of the sectional and laid her bare legs over Ben's lap, enjoying the feeling of his warm hands brushing over her skin. She had no pull here; it was her word against everyone else's. As good a time as any to get scared shitless again by another vision, she surmised. "*Fine.* But if I can't sleep, it's on *you.*" She booped Ben's nose, and they shared a tender kiss.

"Eww," Val sneered. Abby tossed a throw pillow at her, and Val scoffed, throwing it right back.

Dustin brushed away a few damp locks of hair from his forehead and asked, "Are we having a girl fight? Because... I'll gladly watch."

The dry looks from Jamie and Ben made him pout and bow his head. *"Damn."* Abby now squealed and hurled the throw pillow at him, which he caught with thanks. Then he sat cross-legged on the recliner opposite everyone, hugging the pillow, and settled in.

"Well, without further ado... I bring you the story of the Clatter Man."

10

THE CLATTER MAN

Dustin leaned forward and began to tell the grim tale, using his hands to emphasize every detail. Val, Abby, Jamie, and Ben listened in a tipsy stupor.

"It all began in the late eighteen hundreds. Charles Blackthorne was the proud owner of a slaughterhouse in New York, and he supplied the best meat in town. Bacon, pork, ham, you name it... if it wasn't from Blackthorne, it simply wasn't good. He was born and raised on a nearby farm—took over the slaughterhouse when his dad Chuck died.

"Now his dad—he was named Charles, too. But everyone liked to call him Chuck. When young Charles took over after his dad died, it took a few years for people to warm up to him. Sure, he was the son of Big Charles. Respect takes time though, ya know? But soon he had that slaughterhouse up and running like it always had been, and he'd proven himself. So he became known as Chuck, too, just like his dad."

"We get it," Ben muttered. "Where's this going?"

"Just—hold on!" Dustin replied. "So *impatient*. You kinda gotta know where this guy came from to understand why he snapped." Ben leaned back again, sighing and gesturing for Dustin to proceed.

"Okay, so... Charles becomes Chuck," Dustin continued. "Slaughterhouse is running great, and the people are happy. All the while, he's been dating a girl named Anna—love of his life. His mom passed when he was little, dad wasn't there for him much, b ut *Anna*. She's his everything. Swept him off his feet, done deal. And she's a beauty. Year or so goes by, and he proposes.

"They end up marrying and have two beautiful kids together. And all's great for a few years. They're really happy. But then one winter, Anna and the kids catch a horrible case of the flu. And remember, this is the eighteen hundreds, so... there's no cure for the flu. Chuck tried his best to nurse his family back to health, but eventually they all passed away."

"That's *horrible*!" Abby cried out. "This poor guy—losing his whole family?"

"Oh, you won't be feelin' sorry for him for *long*," Dustin replied, then went on. "So, this guy loses his whole family to the flu. The love of his life, his young kids... like, what could be worse? He turns to alcohol—I think most would—and becomes a hermit. Doesn't want to talk to *anyone*, doesn't want to be *seen* by anyone. He eventually goes absolutely batshit crazy and releases most of his pigs. Just lets them run free in the New York countryside, lets his slaughterhouse go to shit. And people start to wonder, you know? Like... what is he *doin'* on that farm now? No one hears from him, and his business obviously comes to a halt. But that's when it starts..."

"*What* starts?" Val asked, eyes wide.

"Well, people can be jerks, right? We all know that—look at Jamie here." Jamie sneered and shook his head.

"*Okay, okay*... just kiddin'," Dustin replied. "But seriously, some people in town want to poke *fun* at Chuck now. They get to thinkin' he's a big wuss all holed up in that farm, wasting away. How could he *do* this, just shut down all operations and tarnish the Blackthorne name? So they start to walk by his house and throw garbage on his lawn, knock on his door and do the ole poop in the bag trick. Some even throw rocks through his windows. And soon enough, more people join in. Rumors start to spread like wildfire—Chuck is officially a reject." Dustin paused as his friends motioned for him to continue, then went on.

"Okay... so this goes on for a month or so, and still, no one sees or hears from Chuck. Then someone says they heard he's got business back up and running a bit and is now taking special orders from locals. He's not running on the scale he *used* to be, but his new meat is supposed to be *delicious*. Better than anything anyone tasted before. And the townspeople who ridiculed him? Now they're *begging* to try his new stuff."

"What's so special about his new meat?" Abby asked. "Or, is it... what I *think* it is?"

"Well... let's just say people have started to go missing. The first time it happens to a teen boy, everybody thinks maybe a runaway or something because the police can't seem to find anything. But then it happens again, and again. People start to go missing, one after the other. And there's really no rhyme or reason to it. Young, old, men, women—just runs the gamut, you know? The only pattern is that it's all people from town. All people who were mean to Chuck when he was at his lowest point.

"One day, a group of teenage boys takes it upon themselves to go investigate. They knock on his front door, no answer. Now it's getting dark, so the sun's creepin' down. There's no lights on in the *house*, but there's lights on in the slaughterhouse at the back of his property."

"Don't go to the slaughterhouse... don't *go!*" Val cried out, her fists held up to her face with clenched teeth.

"Well, that's exactly what they do," Dustin replies. "Because this *is* a scary story, after all. Smart moves go out the window." He adjusts himself in the recliner, then continues. "It's a long walk to the slaughterhouse, but the boys need to know what's going on. Is Chuck the reason these people keep going missing? I mean, no one else is doing anything about it. Maybe they can become heroes or something?

"The closer they get, they start to hear sounds. Like... tearing, cutting. Wet sounds. And then they hear something being plopped into a bucket. Now, they start to give ole Chuck the benefit of the doubt. He's just slaughtering one of his pigs. Because... of *course*, right? He can't be slaughtering a damn *human*, for God's sake. And when they get close enough, they see him in the long hallway. His back is to them, and he's a huge guy. Did I not mention that yet?"

Everyone shook their heads, fully entranced in the story Dustin was weaving.

"Okay, so... yeah, he's scary huge. And he's standing in front of something hanging from the ceiling by a hook. His arms are moving back and forth, just going to work on this thing. And the boys cover their mouths with their hands, because they don't want to make a sound, ya know? But one of them steps on a stick. CRACK! All of a sudden, Chuck stops. He stands still, his back still facing them. And these teen boys, their hearts are racing, you know? Like, *shit*! What the fuck's gonna happen *now*? And then, Chuck slowly turns around to face them, and he backs away from what's hanging from the ceiling. You wanna guess what it is?"

"Um, a *person*... duh," Jamie replies.

Dustin points at Jamie. "*Bingo!* There, hanging upside down from the ceiling, is a man who just disappeared a few days ago. He's gutted from neck to groin, just like a pig. Now they have no doubt what's in the bucket. Human organs. Turns out Chuck has been turning the whole goddamn town into cannibals, eating their own. Who knew human meat was so... *yummy*."

"That's *disgusting*." Abby grimaced.

"Yeah." Then Dustin raised his hands in surrender. "But what a way to give it to those townsfolk, amiright? Like, don't fuck with Chuck."

"So what happens next?" Ben asked. "What happens to those boys?"

"*Well*," Dustin continues. "They hightail it outta there! Go home, they tell their parents, and Chuck is later questioned by the police."

"What does he say?" Val asked.

"He tells 'em *exactly* what's been going on. Mocks 'em right to their faces for becoming goddamn cannibals. Big Chuck's got nothing to hide. Serves them right, sons of bitches. They never helped him... never did anything about the vandalism or anything. Never investigated *shit*."

"What happens to Chuck, then?" Abby asked.

"Well, good ole Chuck is eventually sentenced to death by electric chair. Oh, and he *sizzles* all right. The warden who pulls that switch sends so many volts through his body that he burns from the inside out—flames *literally* shoot out from his head. And oddly enough, as he burns to death, wind chimes begin to rattle everywhere in town in unison. People like to say that was his wife and kids, reaching for him from beyond the grave. Hence—the Clatter Man. Wind chimes, cling clatter and all."

"This sounds... I mean, this is an urban *legend*, right? The Clatter Man. It's just... it sounds like this could have really happened back in the day. Like, it's not completely *un*believable," Ben said.

"Well, *you* be the one to judge. But those boys who reported him? They all disappeared without a trace. Never found. Every... last... one of 'em."

"So Chuck's dead. Gets fried. End of story. But what's this about *conjuring* him?" Val asked.

"Yeah." Dustin rubbed his hands together. "Well, that's the part that makes this story *really* creepy. So word is, if you summon Chuck's spirit, he'll come for you and he'll gut you like a pig." Then he shrugged his shoulders. "Or he'll just slit your throat, bash your head in. There's really unlimited options here. Choose your own adventure, right? And if he doesn't get you right away... just wait. Target's on your back." He paused before proceeding. "Oh yeah, and you'll know he's there if you hear wind chimes—telltale sign he's been conjured up."

Val stood up quickly. "Abby, where are your keys?"

"What?"

"Where are your *keys*?"

"*I* don't know. They're... oh, they're in the kitchen. But why?"

Val strode to the kitchen, and the jingling of keys could be heard. She walked back to the group, raising her hand to showcase Abby's keys. "Bingo!"

"But what do you need with my—"

"Be right back!" Val called as she trotted out the door.

"I don't... okay, I'm getting bad vibes here," Abby said, tucking her knees to her chest and wrapping her arms around her legs. Ben cuddled her and chuckled. "C'mon, babe. It's just stupid shit. There's no *Clatter Man*."

Silence fell upon the group as Val reappeared holding the Ouija board in her hands, the one they had used at her cousin's house. She lowered her head and flashed a snarky grin. "Wanna find out?"

11

Fun and Games

"*Seriously*, Val? How was that still in my Jeep? Gives me the fucking creeps!" Abby said.

"Okay, Dr. Seuss." Dustin laughed.

"Oh my God—*shut* it, Dustin!" Abby scoffed.

"C'mon... it's fun!" Val jeered. Then her eyes lit up. "Remember? At my cousin's place? Nothing *happened*. And look..." She pointed to herself and then to Abby. "...we're still alive, right?"

Abby sighed, remembering the vision of Holly she'd seen that night hanging between them. That petrified flesh and sinister grin sent a shiver down her spine. And now they were back in this same goddamned predicament. "Are we *really* doing this again?" Looking at Ben, Jamie, and Dustin, she received nods of lackluster approval. Dustin's nod seemed a bit exaggerated, though.

"No, we're not," Dustin replied. "Because that's not how you *summon* him, Val."

Silence fell heavy on the room, and a tinge of panic trembled in the air.

"Well then," Val spoke softly as she leaned forward, elbows on her knees. "How *do* you? Is it, like, Bloody Mary or something?"

"I mean, *kinda*," Dustin replied. "There *is* blood involved."

"*Okay!*" Ben's voice boomed as he clapped his hands together. "That's a 'No, thanks,' from me."

"No kiddin'," Abby chimed in. "Me, too."

Val grinned, then spoke again. "What do you *mean*, blood involved?"

Dustin rolled his eyes and sighed, settling back into the recliner. "You're supposed to prick your finger, then you draw a 'V' on the mirror in blood while you say his name three times." Then he stretched his arms out to his sides, palms up, and quipped, "There! You happy now? That's how you do it. But we're not going to."

"Why the 'V'?" asked Jamie.

Pursing his lips, Dustin begrudgingly elaborated. "You draw the 'V' because you're invoking five people as you summon him. He's still mourning the loss of his wife and children, and they were a family of four.

The fifth person? That's the one doing the summoning. So it's kinda like a blood pact, in a way."

"A blood pact that's essentially a death sentence," Abby replied.

"Yes." Dustin nodded back in agreement. "For you and everyone else with you. Apparently, there was a blood-drawn 'V' discovered on a mirror upstairs when they were investigating the babysitter murders. Of course, it's just hearsay. But, you know, not something I really want to find out firsthand."

"Well, I do!" Val squealed, jumping up and running to the kitchen. When she appeared again, she held a serrated steak knife in her hand. Before anyone could object, she'd pierced the skin of her pointer finger and displayed the slow trickle of blood to her friends. Then she motioned to the mirror hung on the wall. *"Shall* I?"

"Um. I'd rather you *not*, babe," Jamie responded, echoing the sentiment of the room.

Abby launched up from the sofa to stop this absurd charade, but Val had already turned to the mirror and was drawing the 'V' with her long, thin pointer finger as the slow chant danced from her lips. "Clatterman, Clatterman, Clatterman..."

Abby stopped in her tracks, and Dustin, Ben, and Jamie all stood up. Wringing his hands, Dustin spoke with an air of reproach. "I don't think you should have *done* that, Val."

"Are you fucking serious?" she quipped. "This shit is just made up. You *know* that, right? The whole babysitter murders story. It's just like the Hookman, or any of the others. Just fun scares, nothing more. And see?" She gestured around her now, shoulders hunched up. "Nothing. Literally *nothing* is happening."

No one chose to address Val and instead all gazed at the floor in collective stillness. If they could just wait this moment out, know for sure nothing would happen, then they could move on: case closed.

But in the silence that continued, a slight breeze caressed each of them, and the faint sound of wind chimes could be heard. They all froze, eyes wide and mouths agape.

"Dustin... the wind chimes," Val whispered.

"I... I don't... Maybe there's some wind chimes outside? A breeze?" Dustin replied.

"Um, there was just a breeze in *here*, with no open windows. Explain *that*," Abby replied, wrapping her arms around herself and frowning.

"Guys, *c'mon*. Dustin's right," Ben said. "Probably some wind chimes outside we didn't see before. This is stupid."

They all looked at Jamie, who stood and stared in horror at the mirror on the wall, lips trembling.

"Jamie?" Val said. "Babe, what is it?" She walked over and stood next to him, staring into the mirror now too. "I don't see anything—just us? What are you looking at?"

"He's... he's here."

The words slithered out of Jamie's mouth. All he could see was a large man standing behind him in the mirror, staring back at him. Long, scraggly black hair was loosely pulled back in a low ponytail, and greasy wisps hung at his temples. Though his face was steeped in shadow, Jamie could make out unnatural lines and grooves... sinewy, as if badly burnt. A mischievous grin spanned from cheek to cheek, and the man's sinister white eyes sparkled in the moonlight as his chin grazed Jamie's right shoulder. One hand rested on Jamie's left shoulder as the other was suspended in front of his neck, grappling a meat cleaver. Though the large, rectangular blade was aged and blotted with rust, the cold steel still shone bright. And the edge of the blade was razor sharp, just beckoning to part his delicate flesh.

12

SECOND THOUGHTS

"*Jesus Christ,* Ben! I know what I saw!" Jamie screamed.

"Just... calm down, man." Ben stood in front of Jamie next to the dining room table, holding his hands up, palms facing his friend in a pacifying gesture. "We got spooked... everyone's on edge right now. Your mind is probably playing tricks on you."

Jamie furrowed his brow and shook his head. "You don't know what I saw." He pointed at the mirror with a savage look in his eyes. "He was *right* there. Standing behind me with a goddamn *meat* cleaver to my throat!"

Dustin leaned his head back as he sat at the table, staring at the shadows dancing along the ceiling. The downpour outside had now settled to a serene rhythm, and, closing his eyes, the sound began to resemble tiny drumbeats in his swirling head. He wondered if he'd taken this too far. What had begun as a fun idea had now created a surge of panic in everyone, and his spinning mind wouldn't settle. He'd opened up a new stash of weed tonight to celebrate. Weed he'd bought from his buddy, who warned him it was strong shit, and... that was *it*! Of course, because Jamie had smoked a ton of it earlier tonight. And he didn't smoke up that much to begin with.

"*Jamie*, Jamie." Dustin chuckled. "Don't you realize?"

"Realize *what*?"

"It's the fuckin' *weed*, man. I opened a new stash tonight. Supposed to be strong shit, and, I mean—*I'm* doing okay. But you smoked a *shitload* outside, my friend. Giving you some... hallucinations." He swirled an index finger by his temple as he said this.

Jamie placed his hands on his waist and shook his head. "Fuck. I don't even know what to think anymore. I mean..." He closed his eyes tight and winced before opening them again. "It was *so* real! Like... I *swear* I'm not making this shit up, man."

"We *believe* you," Val said, stroking his hair with her long fingers. "But Dustin's right—you were smokin' that shit like a chimney tonight! It's all in your head, babe." She lightly booped his forehead with her finger.

"I don't know, I mean... I guess," Jamie said. "Hell, we're all in one *piece*, right?"

"That we are," Abby agreed, nodding her head. Relief had washed over her now—having not seen a vision, she felt recomposed and levelheaded. "And now we can move on from this ridiculous *game*. Right, Val?"

Val was still standing by Jamie with a look of concern. "I... Yeah, we can move on."

Abby sighed, tilting her head and staring back at Val. "Maybe our senses have all been compromised in some way?" Then she glanced at Dustin. *"Hmm?"*

He shrugged. "I mean, *sure*. Just some... subconscious thing going on." He looked over to Jamie. "It's nothin', man. Just your mind playing tricks."

Ben nodded to Dustin, then supported his theory. "It's raining outside, we have some candles burning, the lights are dimmed... Dustin's fuckin' stank-ass *weed*. I mean, we're practically *telling* ourselves to make shit up. Let's just move on."

Val pursed her lips and nodded, grabbing the Ouija board from the table. It felt different now. *Heavier*. Putting the board back in the box, she placed it in one of the lower kitchen cabinets, out of sight.

"I don't know about you guys, but I'm tired," Abby said. "This whole spooky shit has got me trippin'. You all can stay up longer if you want, but I'm out."

"Abby, I'm sorry!" Val scampered to her friend and held her hands. "I feel like I ruined the whole night."

"It's okay, Val. Not your fault. Maybe your *cousins'* for putting all this scary shit in your brain... but not yours."

"No bad feelings, then? We're good?"

"We're good," Abby replied, squeezing Val's hands.

Val smiled sweetly and beamed at Abby. "Okay. Well... if you're turning in, then I will too."

"Yeah, let's call it a night," Ben said. Then he pointed at Val. "And no more weird shit tomorrow."

Val lowered her head to the floor and held one hand up in surrender, palm facing Ben. "No more."

13

NIGHT SCARES

Dustin awoke in his bed in a cold sweat. Breathing in a sharp, deep breath, he looked around the room, examining every dark corner. He had the uncanny feeling he was being watched, but ultimately chalked it up to his imagination from the night's shenanigans. Placing his palms to his cheeks, he ran them down his jawline and his neck, breathed out, and lifted his head to the ceiling. Then he froze.

There was something slithering along the ceiling. Ripples danced along the surface, and his jaw dropped open. This had to be a dream. This couldn't be real. Every so often, something would try to break through. Some kind of... limb. An arm? A leg? He couldn't quite tell. And just as soon as it had jutted out, it flattened into itself again. What the hell *was* that? It wasn't... It *couldn't* be... Dustin slapped himself on the cheek, hoping to awaken from this nightmare. But there was no change. He didn't jolt awake. He just lay in bed, staring at the ceiling that had now returned to a normal state. Aside from the sweeping shadows the full moon cast along the flat surface, there was nothing.

Closing his eyes, he sighed and pressed his fingers to his forehead, furrowing his brow. He needed a drink... something cold. His head was throbbing. Flinging the sheets off himself, he swung his legs over the side of the bed and sat there, palms pressed into the mattress. He'd left the door to the basement bedroom open and could see into the entertainment room. The pool table was bathed in bright moonlight, and the curvature of the billiard balls shone softly in the dim glow. And though the rain had stopped, a slight breeze caressed the trees outside, strewing haunting silhouettes along the walls. Swallowing the lump in his throat, he stood and walked to the doorway. Peering out to the left and right, all was still. No more dark illusions hexing his already fragile state.

He was parched. Couldn't remember the last time he'd drank and smoked this much. But hell, he was vacationing with his friends... all bets were off. Rubbing his hands over his arms, he noticed the temperature had cooled quite a bit since he'd headed in. Stepping back into the bedroom, he grabbed some pajama pants and his Iron Maiden T-shirt, then headed out of the room. There was still that feeling, though. The feeling he was being watched. And it was magnified now that he was in a different state, in a remote cabin, in the fucking backwoods. Sighing, he trudged toward the bar, hoping for a sink where he could get a swig of water. Stepping behind it, no dice. There was a nice little wine cooler with a few wine bottles, but no, thank you. Chilled wine would not hit the spot. *Shit.* He really didn't want to trudge upstairs, but his throat was so dry, and dehydration had set in big time.

Turning to the right, he walked toward the staircase. It was an open staircase, and he peered through the steps at the back of the room before ascending. What was that? Something was in the corner of the room. Something waist-height and... distorted. His heart began to pound, and he stepped back, the adrenaline surging now. It stood still, and had jagged edges; it was... "Oh, fucking hell," he whispered to himself. "A damn plant." Putting his hand to his heart, he leaned forward and chuckled softly. Goddamn Val and her tricks. She'd freaked *everyone* out.

Gaining his composure, he climbed the steps up to the first floor. As he stepped out into the main room, all was silent except for the faint chorus of crickets outside and the unsettling tick of the grandfather clock. Pursing his lips, he headed toward the kitchen, rounding the grandfather clock as he did so.

That thing freaked him out. Sure, it made a statement. It was unique, and cool, and scary as all hell at three in the morning. What was it about three in the morning? Wasn't there some kind of saying about this hour? Oh yes, the witching hour. Seemed appropriate right now.

Heading to the cabinets, Dustin grabbed a glass and went to the sink. As he moved the faucet handle to cold and began filling the glass with the refreshing water his body craved, he caught something in his peripheral vision. Looking toward the right, he saw the Ouija board on the table. It had been unboxed and was lying on the tabletop with the planchette set upon it. He remembered Val boxing it up and putting it in a kitchen cabinet. He remembered the utter horror on Jamie's face as he stared into the mirror. He remembered... what was that trickling down his hand?

Looking back to the sink, he saw the water had begun to overflow now. Turning off the faucet, he breathed in slow and deep, then glanced at the Ouija board again, frozen in fear. He couldn't move—every limb surged with adrenaline, yet his muscles were tense. He was waiting for something... anything. But there was nothing. Just him, the crickets, and the grandfather clock.

A light scratching sound emanated now in the darkness as the planchette darted over an inch, then stopped.

Run!

Dustin booked it downstairs, slammed the door behind him, and drank what little was left of the water in his glass. Sleep escaped him that night, as did any sanity he felt he still had.

14

PRESENCE

The two small wooden crosses hammered into the thick soil of his backyard stared back at him now against the low-hanging clouds. He had affixed them over the graves of his two young children just two weeks ago. Everything in his peripheral vision began to dim as he traced the curvature of the oak tree branches he had nailed together. They seemed to dance with vigor just as his son and daughter had, yet ultimately represented the absolute permanence of death.

And now his Anna had succumbed to sickness, too. He wondered how much time he had left with her. In the face of death, one wishes for a crystal ball but also fears what truth it will speak. And so it came down to this... tending to her every need, and praying to the same God who took his children from him to spare the love of his life.

He wished he could implode on himself, if only for a little while. Remove the pain eating at his every nerve and replace it with... nothingness. Feeling had become a burden in itself. Looking to the ground, he exhaled and noticed the small pin-sized dots accumulating on his leather shoes. It had begun to drizzle. And he smiled, thinking of how his kids loved to dance in the rain, lapping up raindrops as if they were sugar—all rosy cheeks and laughter.

Then he heard it... a guttural moan that floated through the open window of their bedroom coming from a voice he had memorized every inflection of since they'd first met so many years ago. *Anna!*

Her mournful lament cut through the air, and once again, his every muscle tensed with fear and adrenaline. Looking back to the house, he turned and ran as fast as his legs could carry him. He had already lost his two beloved children, Patrick and Susie; he was not going to lose her, too. If God had any mercy at all, He needed to damn well prove it.

Yanking the front door open, he turned on his step and ran up the stairs to the right, lungs on fire now with a fierce mix of dread and determination.

"Anna!" His voice crackled, consumed with anguish. "Sweetheart, I'm here!"

Their room was at the end of the long hallway—a hallway that now felt dizzying and mesmeric. Death had already clenched Anna's heart, and its dank aura fell heavy upon him now. Entering the room, he saw her lying on the bed as she had been the past few weeks, drenched in sweat. Her emaciated figure was visible under the covers, and his chest tightened at the sight of her now.

She was his everything: the sun rose and fell around her. While others had abandoned him, her love had always been pure and steadfast. As he softly placed his hand on her cheek, she looked up to him with those beautiful blue eyes that had lost their spark; their vibrance muted, they now reflected a somber acceptance. Stroking her soft blonde hair, he then caressed her forehead, running his fingers gently to her temple.

Her lips turned up slightly at the corners, but then her eyes became heavy, and she winced in pain. When the lithe scream grew to a throttle from Anna's fragile core, Abby's eyes shot open... and she realized they weren't alone anymore.

15

I Got a Bad Feeling

The next day hung thick with trepidation for Abby, and she couldn't shake the dream she'd had last night. She could almost feel the man's presence now. It seethed with vengeance, yet had a soft tinge of melancholy.

She sat on the backyard patio looking out at a dusky sunset, taking small comfort in the sturdiness of the wooden Adirondack chair. It had begun to rain again, and the soft pitter-patter of droplets on the patio cover above her was soothing.

The rest of them were inside preparing dinner, and she could hear their carefree laughter amidst the clanging of pots and pans. Pasta tonight with homemade tomato sauce, and she didn't feel one pang of hunger. What she *did* feel was the disquiet that had been gnawing at her psyche all day. It had been especially ravenous during the serene afternoon spent sunning by the lake. So much for a relaxing vacation… she was mentally exhausted.

The sliding door behind her opened, and, looking up, she saw Dustin smiling down at her. A light wisp of nervous butterflies began a flurry in her stomach, and she readjusted herself in the chair, hoping he hadn't noticed how quickly she'd averted her gaze. She'd never had a poker face, and that surely wouldn't go unnoticed.

Contrary to her original hesitation, she'd enjoyed having Dustin here now. His off-the-cuff humor was endearing, and he made everyone feel, well—relaxed.

"Mind if I join you?" Dustin asked.

Smiling and nodding her head, Abby replied, "Sure."

He sat down next to her, and she looked at the ground, then shot him a timid glance.

"Welp," he said, raising his hands, then slapping his palms on his knees, "We're all still here, huh? To be honest, I wasn't a big fan of Val doing what she did last night. This kinda stuff just freaks me out, you know?"

"Yeah, me too."

"Listen," Dustin replied in a subdued tone. "I heard the story about your roommate, the one who got murdered. And… I know some people don't believe what you saw. But I do."

"Thanks. Yeah, Ben and Val have always been a bit skeptical. Half the time, I don't even believe *myself*, but... she's not the only ghost I've seen." Abby paused, then continued, "I saw one the night of the séance, at Val's cousins' place."

"Pretty freaky." Dustin chuckled with unease.

"Yeah, it's fucking terrifying." Abby paused, considering her next words carefully. Pivoting to face Dustin, she asked, "Hey, can I tell you something and you promise not to think I'm crazy?"

"Shoot—I'm all ears. And I won't think you're crazy. You don't gotta worry about that. Besides, I think we're all a little crazy."

Smiling, she took a big breath in, then sighed before continuing. "I had this dream last night. And..." She shook her head, unsure of whether to go on.

"What?" Dustin asked, leaning his weight toward her with concern in his eyes.

"Well, in this dream. I *swear* it was the Clatter Man. I saw a snippet of his life when his wife was dying, and... I feel like, somehow, I'm connected to his wife. In some..." She squinted her eyes and moved her hands as if mimicking wheels turning. "...in some weird way." Dustin just listened, eyes growing sorrowful now, and she hoped he wasn't taking pity on her. "And now," she continued, "I feel like he's here. And shit's about to hit the fan."

Dustin was still silent, but there was something he wanted to say too; she could see it festering in his muddled expression.

"What? What is it?"

"It's... it's nothing," he replied, scratching his wavy locks. He didn't want to add more fuel to the fire. Besides, his memory of last night was so hazy, and what he'd experienced must have been a bad dream. *Had* to have been. No one had mentioned anything unusual about the Ouija board, either. It still had to be in the cabinet.

"I don't think you're crazy," he replied. "And I don't think we have anything to worry about. I mean, hell—he's supposed to strike on the first night. At least they do in the movies, right?"

"Yeah, I guess..." she whispered back. Biting her lower lip, Abby then reconsidered as she thought of her dream. This was different, and there were other factors at play she couldn't quite explain. Looking at him with trepidation, she asked, "But what if it's *different* this time?"

"Different *how*?" Dustin asked, leaning toward her as he rested his elbow on the arm of the chair and placed his chin in his palm.

She clicked her tongue and shook her head, shrugging her shoulders. "I don't know. Just... doesn't feel right." When she looked back at him, he was smiling at her with that same warm smile she turned down three years ago, and butterflies began a flurry again in her stomach. "Listen," Abby said softly. "No bad feelings, right?"

"No bad feelings? What do you mean?"

His genuineness made her feel all the more ashamed, and she knitted her brow before replying. "That time you asked me out, and..."

He waved her thought away with a flick of his hand. "Don't worry about it. No hard feelings. You and Ben make a great couple."

"Thanks. He's a good guy."

Abby wrung her hands in her lap, and Dustin couldn't help but notice how distraught she was. He wished he could take it all away, but that was Ben's job. Turning his gaze ahead, he watched as evening welcomed itself in. Brilliant golden hues were sinking on the horizon as soft indigo made its murky arrival. And murky was what this evening was beginning to feel like.

"How do you do it?" Abby asked, looking ahead before she turned her gaze to him again.

"How do I do what?" Dustin tilted his head and squinted his eyes, a slight smirk turning his lips up at the corners.

"I don't know. You're so, like, *chill* all the time. Nothing ever gets to you."

Dustin's shoulders rose and fell as he breathed in deeply, then exhaled. "I mean, I was picked on a lot when I was a kid. Messy hair back then, used to wear glasses, and of course the pudge." He pointed to his stomach. "Kids'll make fun of anything." Leaning over, he placed his elbows on his knees, then gazed at her. "And you know what? Made me stronger. If you don't like me, fine. No skin off my back." He flicked his hand, accentuating the indifference he was describing. "Don't got time for that shit. I don't worry 'bout stuff that doesn't matter."

Abby's eyes drooped and she smiled affectionately at him. "I'm sorry that happened to you. Kids can be so cruel. I was always pretty shy, so... yeah, wasn't fun for me either." Then she showcased him with her hands. "Look at you now, though! You're the cool kid. *Everyone* wants to be friends with you, and I can't imagine anyone not *liking* you! You're too sweet!" As she spoke those last words, her cheeks flushed and she caved back into her chair.

Abby felt a pang in her chest, and for a few seconds she locked eyes with Dustin. His gaze was so... *inviting*. She fluttered her eyes rapidly, then looked away, embarrassed.

Her genuine nature was infectious, and Dustin couldn't help but feel a slight swoon. Chuckling, he sat back in his chair to mirror her posture so she didn't feel uncomfortable. Then, turning to her, "Thank you. You're very sweet, too." Looking up to the marbled sky, he took a deep breath in and sighed out slowly. She lifted her gaze to the sky as well, marveling at the pale strokes of lavender and rose.

"It is what it is." Dustin spoke, breaking the silence.

"What do you mean?" Abby asked.

"Oh, just something my dad says all the time. I've kinda picked it up myself. Some things are just set in stone, can't change 'em. You control what you can, and that's all you gotta worry about."

Tears welled in Abby's eyes, and she blinked them away as she looked down at the patio floor. Placing her palms on her thighs, she grazed the hard surface with the soles of her sandals. "My dad used to say that all the time. I mean, he would kinda joke about it. Almost gave it a singsong tune when he said it, ya know?"

"Oh," Dustin spoke in a soft tone. "I didn't want to... well, I didn't want to make you sad?"

"No, it's okay," she replied. "I like it. It's..."—she looked to him and smiled, nodding her head—"it's nice."

Dustin closed his eyes and nodded back, then relaxed into his chair again. "Good."

Content with each other's company, they both looked ahead, enjoying this silent respite before going back inside. Dustin glanced over at Abby, noticing how beautiful she appeared now with her soft features aglow in streaks of amber. She met his gaze and smiled, but it didn't hide what he could sense behind the smooth facade.

    Fear.

16

Hot and Bothered

Jamie's fraught expression was a turn-on to Val—she bit her lower lip, then climbed onto the bed on all fours, peering down at him now with salacious desire. Her soft breasts brushed up against his chest, and he closed his eyes, groaning with vexation.

"What's wrong, babe?" she asked as her fingers trailed down to his limp dick. With an exaggerated pout, she asked, "Don't you want me?"

"Yes! I fucking want you so bad, but... you seriously didn't see that?"

"No. There's nothing here. It's just you"—she booped his nose—"and me. You took care of me, now it's my turn to take care of you."

He looked to his left and right, wriggling his wrists and ankles in the thick leather bondage straps. She hadn't bound him up like this in a while, and she'd done good. Lowering her head, her soft hair caressed his skin as she began to kiss him again, working her way down his navel. All the while, he stared at the dark corner a second time... the dark corner where he had just seen a vision of the man in the mirror. Though he'd only seen him for a split second, his eyes weren't playing tricks on him. It was real all right, down to the sickening curve of a menacing hook he'd seen this time. It had been dangling from a chain looped around the figure's neck.

When Val took him in her mouth, his eyes rolled back in ecstasy as her soft, warm tongue circled his shaft. The nightmarish figure immediately vanished from his mind, replaced with pure euphoria. Bobbing her head up and down, her soft lips felt divine. Then she dropped his now-hardened dick from her mouth, licking her lips, and stood in front of him at the end of the bed.

A black teddy bodysuit in silky satin hugged her gentle curves, pushing up plump breasts, and a garter belt was attached to fishnet stockings that adorned thick thighs. The light of the full moon caressed her soft skin, and he took in every delectable bit of her now, sighing in anticipation.

"You've been a bad boy, Jamie."

"I'll do anything you want. Just tell me." His dick was throbbing now, his body at whim to her every mercy.

"Oh, you're doing just fine," she said, taking him in her mouth again. As he moaned, she did the same, feeling pleasure in his rapture. The stress of this evening, the crippling anxiety: it began to diminish within Val's soft, warm mouth. Jamie's body submitted to her ravenous desire. So much so that when she took his dick out of her mouth again, he sported a toddler's frown.

"Why... why'd you *stop?*" he asked, straining his neck to look at her.

"I gotta go pee. Like... really bad."

"Right *now?*"

"*Yes*, right now!"

Jamie dropped his head back down on the pillow in dramatic fashion.

"Dude, I'm *not* holding this in. I'll get a UTI in like five minutes, so I gotta go."

"*Fine*, fine... Just, hurry back. Okay?"

"*What?*" She cocked her head, and a smug grin spread across her face. "You scared of the *boogeyman*?"

"Quite frankly," Jamie spat, "Yes. I *am* scared of the boogeyman!"

"Oh my God. Get over it!" Val teased. Then she bent down, her ample breasts looking delicious, and licked his cock one more time. Sparks ran up his spine, and he shivered with exquisite pleasure. "Back in a jiffy," she said before scurrying out of the room to head downstairs.

Jamie was left helpless and alone.

Closing his eyes, he focused on his breathing. In and out, in and... what was that sound? A rustling emanated from his left, and in turn his heartbeat began to quicken. It thudded in his ears now. *Ba-dum, ba-dum, ba-dum.* Swallowing hard, he squeezed his eyelids tighter, just praying Val would pop back in and whisk him off to euphoria again. Why the hell didn't he ask her to undo the straps before she left? Because he didn't want to look like a chickenshit, *that's* why. Besides, nothing was going to happen to him... right? But the hand that covered his mouth now was definitely not Val's. It was too large, too rough, and reeked of decay.

Jamie's eyes shot open and a scream struggled to launch into the air, but what came out instead was a low muffle. Next to him stood the figure he had seen in the mirror the other night. The figure Val did not believe he saw in the corner of the room.

The Clatter Man.

Shaking his head left and right did no good; the ghoul's hand was pressed firmly on Jamie's mouth, pushing down hard until his jawline succumbed to the pressure. He felt a tear inside as the joints connecting his upper jaw to his lower jaw popped out of place, resulting in stabbing pain that throttled up to his temples. Eyes wide in panic, he could discern no detail on the figure leaning over him—it was a ghastly silhouette in the dimly lit room.

Jamie tried to break free, twisting his wrists and ankles, but the bondage straps seemed to tighten with every frantic effort. There was a flash of light as the meat cleaver was raised above him, then frigid cold when the cutting edge of the steel touched the delicate skin of his throat. But instead of slicing through, the blade simply rested upon his throat. Waiting, taunting, playing. Jamie arched his back in an effort to escape, but again the straps tightened, and he felt the thick leather begin to cut into his flesh. Another scream readied to soar from Jamie's muffled mouth, the exertion of his lungs propelling it forward, but the sharp steel cutting into his skin now stifled it. Searing pain erupted as the cleaver began to slice through his throat, the blade opening layer by layer of delicate tissue.

As flesh and muscle were slowly severed, tears trickled down Jamie's cheeks. And when his trachea was sliced open, he gasped for air he couldn't retrieve. He was a fish out of water, dying a slow and painful death. Closing his eyes, he felt his warm blood ooze down his skin from the large gash as it pooled into the mattress beneath him.

The searing pain in Jamie's throat had dulled to a numb throb and his vision was beginning to fade, though the crushing pressure was incessant. He looked at the Clatter Man, and it stared into his eyes with an expression of scorn and disgust. It was relentless torture. Intentional. Methodical. Vengeful.

17

RUDE AWAKENING

Abby awoke and looked to her left at Ben, who had now turned onto his side. The master bedroom was dark and quiet, and the soft, plush duvet had welcomed lucid dreams in. She slowly traced circles along his wide, strong back and giggled as he twitched under her gentle touch. Lifting her head over his shoulder, she stared into the distance at the lake. In the dead of night, its presence was a bit unsettling—a dark, watery void. But the moonlight caressing the glassy surface was beautiful, and she found herself being lulled to sleep again as her eyelids began to flutter.

Gently kissing his shoulder, she lay back down and pulled the duvet to her chin. As she did so, something in the doorway caught the corner of her eye. Why was the door open? Surely, they had closed it when they went to bed. Blinking her eyes, she strained to focus now on the figure standing before her. It was a man.

A *large* man. Though shrouded in darkness, she could make out the sickening gleam in his eyes. And the twinkle of something sharp held in his hand.

Abby screamed—louder and harder than she had ever screamed in her life. And she awoke from her nightmare shrieking.

"Abby... *Abby!* What the hell? What's going on?" Ben asked, shaking his head, still half asleep.

"There... right there!" she said, pointing to the doorway. But the man was gone now.

In the silence that followed her words, they both realized someone was still screaming below them. It was Val.

Rushing down the stairs, they ran into Jamie and Val's room to find her shrieking and gripping the sides of her head with her hands. Scantily dressed, she was standing in front of the bed, staring down at it. Following her frightful gaze, they laid their eyes upon the bed now, where Jamie was lying with his wrists and ankles tied to the bedframe. But something was horribly wrong. Jamie's stomach was dark and lumpy, and his head was... skewered onto the bedpost at an obscene angle. A revolting expression had contorted upon his face, and glassy eyes stared back at them with a gaping mouth wide in utter agony.

Abby and Ben tiptoed to the edge of the bed, and Val's screams faded into the background as if underwater. Upon closer inspection, they noticed their friend's stomach had been torn open. What appeared lumpy were his actual organs, flayed and glistening as they protruded from his abdominal cavity.

Abby covered her mouth to prevent the hot acid rushing up her throat from propelling out, but it was no use. She emptied the contents of her stomach onto the hardwood floor. Ben rushed to the black satin robe he saw lying on the floor behind Val and covered her with it, allowing her to sob into his chest as he continued to grasp the macabre scene before them. Shaking his head, his lips quivered and utter shock prevented him from speaking.

"He's real!" Val shrieked. "He's fucking *real*! I... I went to the bathroom downstairs and... I had to go pee, then the dinner we ate, I had to..." She reached her arm out to Jamie in vain. *"Jamie!"*

Her boyfriend's dead eyes stared up at the ceiling as fresh blood continued to trickle from the corner of his mouth. The pointed tip of the wooden post protruded from his cheek.

There was a scampering of footfalls as Dustin ran into the room. "What the...? What the fuck's going on?" He set his gaze upon Jamie's maimed body; Dustin's jaw dropped open and he began to mouth words, but nothing came out for a few horrifying seconds.

"Are you fucking *serious*? This guy is *real*? Holy fucking *shit*, man! I can't... I can't..." Dustin started to pace in circles, punching himself in the head. Then he bent down and covered his face with his hands, sobbing profusely. "It's not supposed to be *real*!"

"We have to leave. *Right* now!" Ben demanded.

"This is all my fault!" Dustin screamed, his eyes bloodshot and cheeks strewn with wet tears. "I did this, guys. I *did* this!"

"No..." Val shook her head. "I did this. I killed Jamie." The words crept from her mouth forlorn, and her knees buckled as she slid from Ben's grasp and fell to the floor, sobbing uncontrollably. Abby wiped the vomit from her chin with the sleeve of the hoodie she had thrown on and rushed to her friend's side, rubbing her back in small circles.

"We don't have time for this right now," Ben said. "None of you are responsible."

"But Jamie!" Val cried.

"We'll talk to the police, try to explain this. Right now, there's nothing we can do," Ben said. "Seriously, we need to get the fuck outta here, or we're next."

He grabbed Val's hand and helped her up. Then they all stepped into the hallway, mindful of every dark corner.

"It's clear," Ben said, and in fluid form, they ran down the stairs to the first floor. He grabbed his keys from where he'd left them on the countertop in the kitchen and looked behind him in haste. Dustin stood bewildered, wearing a ragged T-shirt and boxers, Val looked utterly confused in her black robe, and Abby was staring at him with pleading eyes. In a rush, she had thrown on Ben's hoodie, and it hung down to her knees. Under any other circumstance, he would gush at how adorable she looked. Wearing flannel pants and a T-shirt himself, he pursed his lips and gestured to everyone to follow him.

Then they saw it. A lurking shadow stepped out from behind the open staircase that led to the second floor. It began to walk slowly at first, picking up the pace with each stride. Lucid white eyes blazed from within an otherwise grotesque face riddled with scar tissue and ligaments.

"Run!" Ben screamed.

Their brisk strides echoed off the walls of the sleepy cabin as they raced to the front door. Swinging it open, they ran into the hushed night and headed straight to the Jeep. As they were all about to pile in, Abby looked around and noticed Val was not with them.

"Val? Where the hell is *Val*!" she screamed.

The night had become abnormally cool, and vapor from their breath danced in a feverish mist around them. Panicked, they scanned their surroundings, searching for any sign of Val. Sudden illumination from inside the cabin caught their attention, and all three turned to face the A-frame.

There, dangling upside down just behind the glass visage, was Val. Muffled screams ripped from her core as her palms struck hard against the smooth glass. Her right leg was suspended from the ceiling as every other limb swung aimlessly, resembling a wretched fish out of water.

The Clatter Man stepped out from a shadowy corner and could be seen pursuing Val in the background. There was an audible gasp amongst the three of them.

Val was taking her final anguished breaths now, and her utter demise would be on horrific display.

18

LIGHTS OUT

Something had pierced Val's right foot... something thick. And they soon realized in sheer horror that she was being suspended by a metal chain, at the end of which a hook had been driven through her foot.

"G-g-guys? Holy f-fucking *shit*..." Dustin managed to stutter.

"*Val!*" Abby screamed. Her friend heard her and looked straight at them now, wailing and pounding her hands on the glass. "*No!*"

Blood had pooled to Val's face, and it was clear her spirit was fading. The satin robe she'd been wearing had fallen to the floor, and her beautiful figure was now a mournful display of terror and anguish. Frantic limbs slowed their momentum, and her expression became languid. She opened her mouth as if to say something, and this small utterance turned into a bloodcurdling scream as she was pulled backward by her hair.

Her body nearly horizontal with the floor now, Val's free leg kicked in a freakish manner—almost animalistic. Helpless arms flailed, trying to grab onto something. They pinwheeled in panic, and in shock, her friends stood there gawking at this miserable display.

"Guys, we have to... we gotta *do* something!" Abby cried. "We gotta—"

The glass visage of the A-frame exploded into shards as Val's body propelled through, playing out in sickening slow motion. Glass fragments twinkled, almost beautiful now as they burst forth around her forlorn figure. She was a pendulum in motion, rocking back and forth as the sheer velocity had caused the hook to tear a large gaping wound in her foot.

As she continued to sway, a gush of crimson spurted from Val's throat where a glass shard protruded. Lifting her arms, manic fingers tried to dislodge the shard from her throat. But there was no use... it was lodged in too deep and the sharp edges delivered more damage by slicing her fingers. Arms and fingers soon fell limp, though, as her body expired and she hung lifeless, swinging listlessly from the chain. The only movement now was the crimson life force spilling from her throat.

Behind Val's swaying corpse stood the vile fiend that had been summoned from beyond. His smile mocked as he stared down from within, ever so slightly tilting his head. Then he lifted a ragged finger and pointed at them.

The lights inside went out, and they were steeped in darkness once again, save for the pale moonlight.

***

"Get in... get the fuck in!" Ben screamed.

Abby and Dustin did as they were told, and Ben revved the engine to life. They launched forward as he slammed on the gas, sending gravel flying in all directions. As they hit the smooth pavement of the main road, a collective sigh could be felt. They had escaped that goddamn hellhole and were free. The calm lake was a twilight companion as they sped along.

"Holy shit!" Dustin wailed from the back seat. "What the fuck just ha—"

Sight of the figure stepping onto the road and blocking their path jarred his train of thought. Light from the headlights flooded his ghastly features. Ben jerked the wheel hard to the right, veering them off the road as the Jeep sped toward the lake. Acting quick, Ben slammed on the brakes and the Jeep skidded to a stop, but it hadn't been soon enough. The Jeep crashed into the edge of the water, sending another jolt of panic through all three of them. Shifting into reverse and slamming the gas pedal, all four tires began to spin into the lake bed.

"Fuck!" Ben screamed. "All-wheel drive my ass, this thing isn't moving!"

"It's too muddy, there's no traction." Dustin muttered. "My car. Let's go!"

Flinging the doors open, they all leapt out into the shallow water and fought to catch their breath, eyeing their surroundings. There wasn't much time to recuperate.

"I swear, I'm gonna kill this sonofabitch *myself*!" Ben snarled.

"I don't think that's a good idea," Dustin whispered into the night air as he caught his breath. "C'mon…" He motioned them to follow him. "We gotta move."

Shoes now soaked, they scaled the embankment up to the road with caution, frantically looking around them.

"Where did he *come* from?" Ben asked.

"He's a ghost, he can come from wherever he damn well pleases," Dustin replied.

"Jesus… don't give him any credit," Ben spat.

Dustin pointed to his car in the driveway. "We gotta run for it."

"Wait. My wallet," Ben said. "It's in the center console."

"Who gives a *fuck* about your wallet?" Dustin cried. "There's a goddamn *boogeyman* killing us, one by one!"

"Just... hold on!" As he ran down toward the lake, Dustin and Abby noticed the figure now stepping out from under the shade of a nearby tree, advancing upon Ben.

"Ben!" Abby wailed. "He's coming! Come *back*!"

Ben glanced behind him at the approaching evil, then ran back to Abby and Dustin, panting. "The love letter you wrote me, Abby... was in my wallet."

"Love letter... survival." Dustin leveled his hands up and down in front of him, palms up, as if to balance the value of each. "Yeah, I'd pick the goddamn love letter, *too!*" he screamed. Ben's eyes drooped as he glanced toward Abby, who now beamed a glint of affection at him.

"Um, this is *not* the time, guys," Dustin interrupted.

As the ghoul lumbered up the embankment toward them, they bolted to Dustin's car.

"Please be unlocked... *please* fucking be unlocked," Dustin pleaded. When the door handle succumbed to his grasp and the door flung open, he sighed in brief victory and leapt inside. Looking down to his left, he made sure to unlock all the doors. Abby jumped in the front passenger seat, eyeing him with torrid determination, and Ben jumped into the backseat. Dustin folded down the sun visor, and the spare key fell into his lap.

"Dustin! Fucking *gun* it!" Ben screamed.

With that, Dustin started the engine and shifted into reverse, the Impala obediently tearing backward. Eyeing the road ahead, he then hit the gas pedal. The engine roared into first gear, then second, then—

The figure walked in front of them once again, throwing the chain behind it, ready to aim and strike the hook.

"Fuck you, motherfucker!" Dustin screamed as the engine kicked into third gear and he struck the fiend hard, relishing the thudding sound of impact with wild laughter. Abby looked out the rear window to see the figure rolling in rapid succession on the road behind them, the flailing hook and chain illuminated in the soft light of the moon.

Ben clasped his hands on both sides of his head, eyes wide in utter astonishment, then let out a roar of laughter. He grabbed Dustin's shoulder, shaking it hard as he exclaimed with excitement, "Dustin... dude! You... Jesus Christ, you're a fucking *badass*!"

Dustin chuckled under his breath as he looked in the rearview mirror and met Ben's fervent gaze.

"That's how you fucking *do* it!" he exclaimed, reaching back and fist-bumping Ben. Then, shaking his head, Dustin puffed his cheeks and slowly blew his breath out. "I don't know, guys. You think this is really over? You think that motherfucker isn't gonna keep tracking us down, one by one?"

Brief silence overcame the three of them, then Abby spoke, careful with each solemn word.

"We're safe, for now. Who knows if it's gonna come back or not. If it does, God help us all."

19

A BUMP IN THE ROAD

The turn off of Lakeside Drive quelled everyone's nerves... just a bit. Abby and Ben kept looking behind them, only to observe an empty road bathed in the soft luminescence of full moonlight.

As Dustin drove on, they were reminded again of the barrenness about to envelop them. Wide pastures stretched out for miles on either side, and the ghostly outline of farmhouses could be seen from the road. Some were robust, and others—the ones left to ruin—appeared as colossal skeletons. It was a grim reminder of how isolated they would be for the next half hour or so. But farmhouses were lived in, farmhouses had people: people who could help if their journey home took a dark turn again.

"What the hell are we gonna tell the cops?" Ben asked as they drove on.

"That's literally the last thing on my mind right now, man," Dustin replied. "Better question: Why is that sick *fuck* all of a sudden gone? You can't tell me he just vanished. When you summon him, he comes for everyone. Every goddamn last one of you."

"Thanks, Dustin. This is really lightening the mood," Abby muttered under her breath.

He eyed her with concern, then shrugged his shoulders. "Sorry, it's just... I'm a realist, what do you do?"

"Realists don't believe in this shit," Ben scoffed from behind them. "And yet here you are, while Jamie and Val are both fucking *dead*! Because *you* chose to tell this goddamn story that... that you just *knew* Val would want to prove is bullshit because she just can never *fucking* help herself! And then you tell her not to, because—oh, shit—maybe this is all real?"

"Just shut the fuck up!" Dustin's hands were shaky on the wheel, and he sniffled as the tears rolled down his cheeks, lips trembling. Glancing at Ben in the rearview mirror, he continued. "I... you think I wanted them both *dead*? You think I *wanted* this to happen? The babysitter murders, it was just a scary story! At least I thought it was... But you know what? I never said Bloody Mary or Candyman into the mirror because you just never... fucking... know!"

Ben threw his arms up in exasperation, shaking his head and rolling his eyes. "All I'm saying is you could have just kept your damn mouth shut and—"

"*Stop it!*" Abby cried out, slamming her hands on the dashboard. "Right now, we focus on getting home in one, fucking—"

The loud pop startled all three of them, and Dustin immediately began shaking his head in disbelief, while trying to find the words.

"Dude... seriously?" Ben slammed his head against the headrest.

"Is that what I *think* it is?" Abby asked in a rhetorical manner. She knew it was a flat... they all did. Sighing out in frustration, she sank in her seat while eyeing the surrounding landscape sparsely peppered with structural silhouettes. An odd feeling of claustrophobia began to take hold as she envisioned the darkness slowly caving in on them.

"Yep, and pretty sure I forgot to replace my spare," Dustin lamented as he pulled to the side of the road and shifted his car into park. The three of them sat in silence, staring into nothingness, as the engine continued to idle. Then he turned the ignition key, and silence enveloped the cabin.

Abby couldn't believe how much this trip had spun out of control. It had become an absolute *nightmare*. The thought of Jamie and Val dead seemed so inconceivable, and visions of Val's slack body swinging from the chain played on repeat in her mind. She lost all composure. Bending forward, she cradled her face in her hands and began to sob. Rocking back and forth, her body shook as the absolute horror of it all echoed through each anguished lament.

Dustin and Ben both sat still in a stupor, looking on as Abby continued to process the horrific turn of events. Though they could both feel the intensity of her pain, the night had also managed to render them catatonic. Both boys stared at her through a murky lens, one which feelings could not penetrate. After a few somber minutes, Dustin reached over and rubbed Abby's back with his hand. She tensed up at his touch, then leaned into him. Wrapping his arm around her, he looked in the rearview mirror and locked eyes with Ben. Looking down to the floor, Ben met his friend's gaze again and nodded, happy that Dustin could offer his girlfriend comfort.

As the faint and whimsical cadence of crickets sang all around them, here they sat—the three survivors of a slaughterhouse-like massacre. Since their nerves had all been frazzled, it hadn't dawned on either of them what the next step should be. But the realization that the Clatter Man was still hunting them down was very clear.

Dustin stared at the dark road ahead as warm tears trickled down his cheeks; he still blamed himself for everything. Ben was right... should have kept his damn mouth shut. He looked down at Abby, whose head was nestled under the crook of his arm, and stroked her hair. It was so soft to the touch and, closing his eyes briefly, he enjoyed this tender moment. When he opened them, Dustin noticed Ben's stone-cold stare from the rearview mirror and quickly lifted his hand from Abby's hair.

Existential dread had fallen upon the three of them now, and they knew they had to move. Stalling any longer rendered them sitting ducks, the next for slaughter.

"Do you see anything?" Dustin asked Ben. "Out the back... do you see anything?"

Abby rubbed her eyes and lifted her head from Dustin's gentle embrace. They exchanged a brief glance, and she saw him in a different light now. He wasn't just the aloof joker; he was warm, caring, and... *cuddly.* Processing all of these random thoughts in rapid succession, she blinked her eyes, then returned to reality. Turning back to look at Ben, she noticed his hand clenching the corner of her seat as he looked through the rear window. She placed her hand on his, and he quickly turned around, meeting her trembling gaze with one that offered a shaky form of solace.

Placing his palm on her cheek, Ben asked, "You okay, babe?"

"Yeah, I'm... well, no. I'm definitely not okay. But managing."

Nodding, Ben leaned forward and pressed his forehead against hers. In the awkward silence that followed, Dustin cleared his throat and settled back into his rightful place as being the third wheel. Looking out the rearview mirror, he observed the light fog that had begun to settle on the dismal landscape; the meandering road behind them disappeared into a smoky veil.

Turning around again, Ben gazed through the rear window. "I don't... I don't see anything. I mean, it's hard to see much back there, but... nothing. Just the fog."

Abby surveyed their surroundings again, fighting the suffocation of false safety that was seeping in and threatening to quell any sign of hope. Then she saw it... the ominous stone building they had passed on the way here. It was the only structure clearly visible now, the other buildings all being at least a mile away. Mocking them, it stood a menacing presence that was their only shot at survival. They needed to contact help, and there had to be a phone in there.

20

INSTINCT

Vulnerability fell on each of them as they stepped out of the car into the night air once more. With shoulders hunched, they scanned their surroundings for danger... but there was nothing. Rolling farmland and the long stretch of empty road were tranquil companions, and all was silent save for the mournful hooting of an owl in the distance. Standing in unison, they gazed upon the building before them. Its dark silhouette set against the somber night sky was the epitome of a bad omen. While collectively pondering their situation, a scant breeze carried with it the smell of rotting manure, and pungent sweetness flooded their nostrils.

"Well, shit. *That'll* wake you up!" Dustin scoffed, mimicking a gag reflex.

"Welcome to the fuckin' *boonies*," Ben retorted. "I mean, there's a farmhouse like a mile down the road. Why don't we head there?"

"I dunno, that's pretty far," Dustin replied. "Just, gimme a sec. Lemme make sure we're really fucked." He popped the trunk open, then closed it after a few seconds. Opening his hands, palms up, he shrugged his shoulders. "Yeah, we're fucked. No spare."

Abby pursed her lips and placed her hands on her waist, looking at the ground as she considered their situation. Then she gazed back at Ben and Dustin. "I don't know if we should risk the farmhouse. But sure, we could—"

There was a snort, and all three of them looked ahead to see the group of pigs once again congregating in the fenced-in pasture of the adjoining property.

"Funny, those little guys. They're always out, aren't they?" Dustin remarked.

Abby smiled. "Yeah. Cute." She reached her hand out, and one of the pigs lifted its snout. With her fingers, she gently brushed its cool and rough skin. The pig responded with happy grunts, and Abby giggled.

Dustin raised his eyebrows, shaking his head and scratching the back of his neck. "Okay, I mean... this is cute and all, but we gotta make a plan."

"I say the farmhouse," Ben replied, then pointed at the dilapidated building. "I don't wanna take our chances in that shithole. Place looks like it's straight outta hell."

"I'm game," Abby replied.

Abby and Ben looked to Dustin, who shrugged his shoulders and nodded his head. "Fine. Bit of a walk, but... best option right now."

Ben clapped his hands. "It's decided, then. Let's go."

Patting the pig's snout one more time, Abby nodded, and they all began the slow trek to the farmhouse. Though adrenaline had gotten them this far, hunger and fatigue were setting in now that they'd had a moment to let their guard down and collect themselves.

"Dude, I could go for a pepperoni pizza so bad right now," Dustin mumbled. "I'm so fuckin' *hungry*!"

"Yeah, me too," Ben said. "I don't think we're gonna get any *pizza* tonight, but I'll eat just about anything."

"It's the stress," Abby said under her breath. "I'm hungry, too."

They continued on in silence, each labored step feeling so mechanical and tedious. A familiar sound made Abby stop in her tracks, and she cocked her head to the side. Dustin and Ben noticed and stopped as well. Looking toward her, they both shrugged their shoulders in confusion.

"What?" Ben asked. "Why'd you stop?"

"You don't hear that?" Abby replied.

Dustin's brow tensed, but then he leaned his head back, mouth slack in a moment of clarity. "It's the pigs."

"Yeah," Abby replied. "But why are they all the sudden making sounds now? They were pretty quiet before."

All three turned to look at the pigs, which were grunting in unison. Their breathy chorus started as soft and friendly, then began to increase in pitch until they were all squealing in panic. Raising their heads, their ears flattened as they bleated into the sky. And in a mad dash, they raced toward the farmhouse.

"*What* the..." Dustin whispered.

Abby's heartbeat began to race again and she struggled to steady her shaky breathing. The fact that there were no other beings around except for these harmless pigs had felt like a good thing: a *safe* thing. She'd thought all they had to do now was—

"Wait." Ben's tone was laced with panic.

"*What?*" Dustin asked, shaking his head. "What the fuck's going on? Why are these pigs all freaking out?"

"I see something. Oh... oh shit, man. We gotta run. That's him! That's fucking *him!*" Ben's voice cracked as the words tore from his throat, every fractured syllable slicing through the night air.

Dustin and Abby both looked toward the road, where Ben's gaze had settled, squinting their eyes for focus.

A hulking figure was visible through the fog now, walking toward them heavy-footed with shoulders slumped. The outline of the cleaver it was carrying could be seen in its right hand, and something curved in shape gleamed from where it hung around its neck when a slant of moonlight filtered through the haze… the hook.

21

MAD DASH

"What the fuck do we *do*, man?" Dustin winced as he shook his hands in panic, his body shuddering with each trembling inhale.

Their brief respite had crumbled, safety once again seeping through their fingers.

Target's on your back. The words Dustin had uttered earlier tonight danced in Abby's ears again. "We don't have a choice." Her speech wavered but caught solid footing. "That building. We gotta make a run for it."

Dustin shook his head in disbelief as he spoke. "Ah, shit... are you fucking *kidding* me? Kinda wanted option two."

"Dustin, just shut the fuck up and let's go. Now!" Ben's voice boomed.

Taking one last look behind them at the figure closing in, they sprinted to the looming building in the distance. It seemed unfathomably far away, and every stride felt for naught; they just couldn't close in. Lungs on fire, each glanced back intermittently to see the figure following their path. It walked so slowly, so methodically. A crawl, almost. But it was determined; and though there was no end in sight to this nightmare, they had to keep going. Giving up now was not an option.

Running to the nearest door, Ben flung it open. And as they all stepped inside, the foul odor was the first to hit them.

"Oh my *God*. That *smell*!" Dustin cried out as he covered his nose with the back of his hand. The stench was so powerful it burned their lungs when inhaled. A tinge of sweetness drowned by putrid rot seared their nostrils and throat.

Windows flanked the right wall above them, leading down a long hallway. Two rolls of narrow poles led in succession down the hallway as well, at the end of which there was an open doorway. What looked like strewn hoses carelessly snaked along the concrete floor.

"Dude, what the hell *is* this place?" Ben asked as they stepped over hoses and loose boards.

"I don't know," Abby answered. "We gotta find a phone, though. C'mon." She pointed to the doorway in front of them. "Let's go."

Entering the doorway, they were forced to turn left as walls abutted the front and right of them. What greeted them upon entry was a massive room that had a high ceiling and was filled with holding pens. Large square tiles lined the floor, covered in dark grime. The smell of feces was now stronger than ever, and Abby gagged at the pungent stench. Light from the full moon filtered through small windows, bathing everything in a soft glow. Glancing around, there was not a phone in sight. Not even a desk of some sort. Just a succession of holding pens. Another doorway was in sight at the end of the room, and, hoping for the best, they walked through and realized it was a short hallway.

This building was much larger on the inside than it looked on the outside, and the interior was dizzying. What if they got lost and couldn't find their way back? They'd be stuck in this hellish tomb of feces and rot. But there had to be a phone; they had to be able to reach out for help. The sound of cumbersome footsteps echoing now in the nefarious gloom caused goosebumps to pepper their skin. Death was on their heels, and they had to act fast.

Pointing ahead of them to another doorway, Ben nodded his head, and Abby and Dustin both followed his lead. They each made sure to tread with extra care so that nary a sound reverberated off the walls. Did it really matter, though? They were being hunted by a paranormal entity. It may even have the ability to see through walls for all they knew. But caution still had to be used; they couldn't get sloppy.

The next room had a much more sinister feel than the first two, and a large contraption sat in the back corner. A long metal bar with multiple grips (about ankle width)—each about a foot apart—led into the contraption, which housed a tall vertical opening. The sides of the contraption were solid, and what existed within that tall, vertical opening could not be seen. It was a black abyss.

"Guys. I think this is some kind of slaughterhouse," Abby said. "It's not in use now, but I mean... holy shit, what else would this all *be* for?"

Dustin shook his head in disbelief as he spoke. "You gotta be fucking *kidding* me. A slaughterhouse? The Clatter Man? Who slaughtered *pigs* for a living? And the car decides to get a flat right goddamn here? No *wonder* those pigs were screaming. Literally screaming for their lives!"

"Jesus fucking Christ," Ben mumbled under his breath.

Abby bit her lower lip in rumination, then slumped down when she heard the shrill sound: metal scraping against concrete. And it was *close*. He was just toying with them now, feeding on their fear.

"Oh, there's no fucking way! We're done for, guys. This is it!" Dustin whispered, sobbing as he struggled to utter each word.

The three of them looked at each other now, huddled in a small circle, and it was the first time any of them had seen this amount of horror register on their faces. Tears streamed down Abby's cheeks, and Dustin's mouth quivered with fright. Ben was the only one holding it together somehow, but just barely. The sound became faint, ceasing altogether; but in utter terror, they'd succumbed to physical and emotional paralysis.

That's the thing about fear—when you're in its grasp, it can be suffocating. And at this very moment, hope had dwindled to a mere speck. A faint glimmer that there could be a way out of this nightmare still shone, but barely: they'd have to fight tooth and nail. But how do you beat an evil entity summoned from the beyond? Was it even possible?

Still huddled together, they scanned the room, looking for a way out. No other doorways could be seen, though. It seemed the only way out was back through where they had just entered—and this would bring them face-to-face with an inevitable horrifying death. Grim reality set in, and Ben began to say a prayer under his breath. Though Abby and Dustin weren't religious, they reached over and held Ben's hands in theirs, taking solace in what would most likely be their last moments alive.

When the Clatter Man stepped into the open doorway, time stood still as the breath left their lungs. All sound ceased to exist except for the slow echo of footfalls as the hulking entity approached.

While Dustin and Abby stepped backward, scanning the room for any sort of refuge, Ben picked up a shovel lying on the floor and stood tall, facing the ghoul head-on.

"Ben." Dustin's voice wavered with tension. "What are you *doing*?"

"This ends right now," Ben snarled through gritted teeth, facing the figure. "Whoever the *hell* you are, fuckface, I got news for you. You can head back to wherever the hell you came from, or I'm gonna beat the goddamn *shit* outta you!"

"That's not a smart *move*, dude," Dustin whispered, hunkering down next to Abby behind a large wooden crate. Wrapping his arm around her, he drew Abby close.

Sporting a casual grin, Ben looked over to Dustin, who was now shaking his head and urging his friend to join them. "I got this," he assured Dustin. "Just wai—"

Ben was yanked forward in an instant, and the thump of his body colliding against the cold, hard floor reverberated in the dark room.

22

FLICKER

The hook that had pierced Ben's shoulder was embedded under his right scapula, and excruciating pain ignited when his back hit the floor—the firm impact lodging the hook deeper into his flesh: metal sliding through taut muscle. This combined with the back of his head slamming against the concrete rendered him momentarily catatonic. Looking up through wary eyes, he saw the ceiling slowly passing by above him.

He was being dragged backward.

When Ben's senses came to, the sound of metal scraping the floor under him became more apparent, as did the tug on his right shoulder where the sharp point of the hook could now be seen protruding from his gray T-shirt. Slowly raising his arms above his head, he reached back with quivering fingers to touch the cold metal chain, pulled taut. Trying to produce some slack in the chain to alleviate the burning pang in his shoulder rendered itself useless. Lowering his arms now, he tried placing his palms on the concrete to slow this inevitable procession, but it was to no avail.

Lifting his head as best he could, Ben caught sight of Dustin and Abby in his viewpoint, stepping out from behind a wooden crate. Their mouths were moving, but he could only hear muffled noise. The relentless ringing in his ears made it impossible to discern what they were saying, let alone hear much at all.

When the tug on the chain was loosened and his back fell flat against the concrete, Ben pressed his shoes flat against the floor and attempted to prop himself up. As he did so, a large hand gripped his right ankle with firm pressure, and he was lifted upside down. Arms flailing, he looked around the vast chamber in desperation. Spotting Dustin and Abby running to his rescue, a respite of relief fluttered in his heart. They could save him from the Clatter Man. Two against one. Two mortals against an immortal fiend didn't quite offer a fair fight, though. And his hopes were dashed when they began to back away, hands up in defense.

Straining his neck to look up, he noticed the Clatter Man pointing the meat cleaver their way and shaking his head. Ben's heart sank when they began to back off, Abby's face glistening from streaming tears as her mouth writhed in agony. A breath escaped his lungs as

Ben realized he was knocking on death's door: a cruel, punishing door. And the worst was yet to come.

The metal bar they had seen before rested above him like a dark omen now, ready to transport him to the next step in this macabre journey. He was lifted higher, and each of his ankles was clamped into a grip, leaving him squirming in suspension. It was so humiliating—here he was, body strong yet incapacitated and at the mercy of this... his mind raced to the night of the bonfire. Dustin's story, Val's unrelenting dark curiosity. They had done this to him. They'd sealed his fate. And now Dustin stood next to Abby, one hand wrapped around her waist. Ben seethed with anger seeing the two of them now, and jealousy began to boil to the surface. Gritting his teeth, he struggled to breathe, and his vision began to blur as the reverse blood flow added pressure to his lungs and eyes. He opened his mouth to vocalize his vehemence as drool dripped from his lips, but a buzzing sound caught him off guard.

When the grips began to move toward the dark opening, he struggled. Ben seethed now. Dustin should be in his place—how the *fuck* was this happening? He opened his mouth to voice the turmoil he had succumbed to, put into words the absolute torment he felt at this very moment. The roar of fire came to life in the narrow slit his dangling body was being led to, which forced a thunderous scream from his compressed lungs. Terror-stricken, he tried reaching his arms up to the grips but found it impossible to bend his core. Increasing dizziness had rendered him helpless, and at the mercy of the Clatter Man.

Giving in to his fate, he looked forward now to see the massive figure standing before him, still holding the chain in his right hand. Dustin was running up behind it now with a metal rod, ready to strike. But the fiend swung his right arm back wide with remarkable strength, knocking Dustin square in the jaw and ripping the hook from Ben's shoulder. As the metal tore through muscle and bone, breaking through his scapula and clavicle, Ben took a deep gasp in. The searing pain in his shoulder detonated in every direction and shock clouded his vision momentarily, which now pulsated with each heartbeat. When he looked at his right shoulder, the sharp edges of broken bone protruded, appearing stark white against fleshy tissue. It was unrecognizable, and he blinked several times, trying to make sense of what he was actually observing.

As his right side began to feel the heat of the flames he was about to enter, Ben looked ahead of him again and saw the Clatter Man stepping backward now, his head cocked. He enjoyed this sick game. Dustin lay on the floor behind him in a heap, and Abby stood next to the wooden crate, screaming something. What, he couldn't hear. All he could do was mouth the words, "I love you," hoping she would understand.

In Ben's delirious state, the warmth of the fire was comforting at first, but when the scorching blaze came in contact with his tender flesh, the pain was insufferable. Singed nerves shrieked in torment as the fire consumed him. As his body was charred and hot gasses flooded his lungs, the impending suffocation brought respite from this torment.

Ben breathed one last labored breath before his life was extinguished.

23

CLASH

"Ben!"

Abby's voice cracked as she cried out, watching Ben's suspended body being led into a fiery furnace. He mouthed what looked like "I love you" before the flames consumed him and his excruciating screams pricked her with each tormented wail. Her only solace was when Ben's screams were no more; his torture was over.

Dustin lay on the ground in front of her now, knocked out from the Clatter Man's explosive blow. Was he dead? In the murkiness of the expansive room, it was impossible to tell whether he was still breathing.

The Clatter Man stood motionless, eyeing the furnace that had just taken her boyfriend's life. In an instant, the torture device was shut off somehow, and silence pervaded the room. As she stood there, shuddering and clenching her fists, the massive figure ceased to move. No rise of the shoulders, nothing… lifeless, just like the void of what used to be a human heart.

Dustin began to moan as he rolled his head back and forth. Abby knew time was running out, and she had to act now or they'd both be goners. Looking around her, she spied the metal rod that had flown out of Dustin's grip as he was knocked out. Heart racing, Abby tightened her lips and knitted her brow. *Now or never.* Launching from her step, she scrambled to the rod and picked it up, then turned to the fiend.

He was facing her now, his fiery eyes locked on her wavering stare. The cleaver in his grip gleamed ruin when a flash of cold steel shone from the moonlight filtering through ceiling windows. Yet there was a hint of sadness in those ancient eyes.

Abby's chest heaved and fell, and she murmured a prayer to herself just then—Ben's prayer hadn't helped, but maybe this one would? If there ever was a time to pray again, it was now. It floated upward from her lips as warm tears streaked her cheeks. She hoped if there was a God, He would spare her and Dustin.

As if in a mocking nature, the fiend made no movement still. Was it waiting to destroy this prayer? Surely it had been called from the depths of hell, so there must be some semblance of heaven, *right*?

Deafening silence fell again upon the room when she had finished her prayer, and a thumping heart beat in her chest. It felt as if it would practically burst from the rush of adrenaline filling every fiber of her being. Raising the rod, ready to strike, Abby struggled to compose shaky legs as she prepared to rush the evil entity.

Rather than charge her, the Clatter Man instead grabbed Dustin by the neck, lifting him from the ground and holding her friend directly in front of him. The top of Dustin's head glistened amid the soft light pouring in, and Abby quickly realized he was bleeding—his head had hit the concrete hard.

Dustin clawed at the massive hand clenched around his throat and struggled to kick the Clatter Man. Abby couldn't lose him, too. *Fuck this piece of shit.*

Taking in a few deep breaths, Abby then lunged toward the ghoul, the metal rod held up in a wild fury to strike down on it anywhere—everywhere. The fiend dropped Dustin to the floor, where her friend kicked his legs and clutched his throat, gasping in labored breaths and welcoming air into his lungs again.

"Fuck you!"

Abby walloped the Clatter Man's back so hard, the contact reverberated through her entire body. She struck it again and again, a savage cry escaping her throat now, tearing up and out like shards of glass. But nothing was happening. The fiend was not faltering under her blows. Raising the rod again as it turned its head now to face her, she prepared for another blow when her arm began to rain down on its countenance. Time seemed to stand still just then as she locked eyes with the beast. Its expression screamed hot rage, but something else pervaded the wretched gleam in its eyes. Something... almost mournful. In one swift movement, it swept its arm to her stomach and sent her flying to the floor.

She hit the ground hard, but thankfully her head hadn't snapped back against the unforgiving concrete. Groaning, Abby placed a hand to her back. Hot pain was radiating outward from her spine, and she clenched her teeth to power through each relentless throb. A metallic clang startled her, and she looked over to see The Clatter Man pacing toward Dustin, who was scooting away from the fiend on the concrete floor. The Clatter Man again swung the cleaver down, and this time it landed right next to Dustin's head. His mouth gaped in terror as he eyed the menacing blade that had nearly split his skull in half. Then, acting fast, he scrambled to his feet and ran toward Abby. But there was a sharp, wet sound. Dustin's face twisted as he stumbled to the floor, the cleaver jutting from his back.

"No!"

Phlegm flew from Abby's throat as she screamed, and defeat began to take hold—every muscle in her body succumbed to it, softening under its dark embrace. It would just be easier, wouldn't it? She was tired, sick of fighting. A flash of acceptance burst into her head, and she took hold of it.

"Take *me*!" Abby screamed. "I don't want to live this nightmare anymore! Take *me*!"

The words flew out; she didn't have a choice. All she knew was that this needed to end—and since she was the next to go, so be it.

The Clatter Man leaned over, yanking the cleaver from Dustin's back. Somehow, some way, her words had gotten through. Dustin had not made a sound, and his body lay lifeless on the floor. Visions of his dimpled smile flashed in her mind now, and her heart sank.

The ghoul rose to stand before her, and the silhouette of its hulking body was made all the more menacing in the twilight of the room. Soulless eyes flared from within the murky gloom of this death sanctuary.

And all Abby could think was... *Run!*

24

Dark Lucidity

The sound of her frantic footfalls was all that could be heard as Abby sprinted to safety, backtracking through the maze of ghastly chambers they had just passed through earlier. When she arrived at the final room, the hoses strewn along the concrete floor were the most welcome sight she'd seen all evening. A subtle wave of relief eased tense muscles as she sprinted this last dash.

Warm summer air that lingered with a hint of mischief surged into Abby's lungs when she'd escaped into the outside world once more. She couldn't believe she was the lone survivor of this horrific massacre. But it wasn't over yet... she needed help, she needed a phone, she needed—

The Clatter Man emerged from the doorway, head bowed and fiery eyes fixated on her. Hanging around its neck was the metal chain, with the brazen hook that had brought demise to her friends appearing contemptuous.

It was almost surreal, this scene before her. The fog had begun to lift, and a glorious full moon shone in an otherwise bleak twilight sky. Fitting for her last night on earth. At least her spirit would rise to meet the full moon above.

The cleaver, smeared with Dustin's fresh blood, was sure to bathe in her blood next. As the Clatter Man stepped toward her, it stopped just feet in front of her. Utter terror prevented her from running, and looking around her as she backstepped, she was greeted with sparse farmland once again. The cozy outline of remote farmhouses against the afterglow called out to her; if only they were closer.

"I... I..." she sputtered, not quite sure what to say. Did it even talk? Or had it become speechless once its mortal life was exhumed? Her mind raced as it stood before her now, and she reached for a bargaining phrase... something that could buy her more time. She could seek to somehow reach the sorrow she'd seen in its eyes. Abby thought of the family he had lost. He must have still loved them after all these years. She recalled the dream she'd had at the cabin, where she could feel the immense love he had for his wife.

If she could tap into that, maybe she'd be able to save herself.

Standing face-to-face, Abby realized this was the first time she could really observe his ghastly features. He was massive, with steely hands as big as bear paws—one of them still gripping the handle of the crimson-stained cleaver. He wore a tattered, black frock coat that ran down to his ankles. A light-colored tunic with a lace front closure could be seen underneath, now almost entirely stained with the blood of her friends. Frayed at the ends, the tunic hung over dark trousers. His dress appeared odd at first, but then she remembered the era he had lived in.

Greasy black hair streaked with gray was pulled back, revealing the horrors of his demise. That face—she couldn't look away. It seemed to still be writhing in pain, with strewn ligaments visible under scathed skin. His jawbone shone within a deep tear along his cheek, and rotten teeth sat within putrid gums. But those eyes... they were still tinged with sadness. He stepped forward now, and she continued to backstep with her hands held up in defense.

"I know who you are," Abby said, trying her best to control her trembling speech. "I know what they did to you. You lost your family, and they treated you like... well, it was *horrible* what they did to you! I understand why you... why you killed them." Lying through her teeth, she said, "I would have done the same."

He cocked his head now. Was she getting through?

"Your wife. Your wife's name was... Anna." As she spoke the name, his brow furrowed slightly, and he snarled. She backed up again. "Losing her must have been so horrible! *Beyond* horrible! Heart ripped out of your chest. And your kids? To lose them so *young*? But they wouldn't want you to do this in their names. They wouldn't want you to... to *kill* like this."

Then he spoke, with a voice from the grave. It rose from deep inside him, thick and gravelly.

"Anna."

"Yes, Anna!" Abby exclaimed, smiling at this connection. She had reached through to whatever human still resided in him somehow.

"You look like... Anna," he said now, slowly advancing again.

"Oh... no, no," Abby responded, waving him away. "I'm not Anna." She pointed to herself and felt like a child now. "I'm *Abby*."

He groaned and seemed to vaguely consider her words.

When she saw a light turn on at the farmhouse a lot over, a sharp inhale accompanied blissful hope. It was practically a mile away, but—did she even have a choice? Puffing her chest out, she readied herself. This was it. Keeping a steady eye on the Clatter Man, Abby hoped she hid the hot surge of energy that was pumping adrenaline through every limb right now, readying her for the race of her life.

One... two... three!

Abby bolted to the farmhouse, sprinting as fast as she could to reach the safety of that soft light. Waving her hands in the air, she began to scream, lungs on fire. Absolute elation spread over her face as she smiled wide, and untamed laughter erupted from deep within her lungs.

The touch of a large hand clamping the top of her head froze her mid-stride, and though her breath was still racing, she'd succumbed to paralysis. Panicked, her eyes darted in a frenzy in all directions as the adrenaline still coursed hot through her body. But she was frozen, unable to move as much as a finger.

"Remember me..." The words were whispered ethereally behind her, rising from a place of fathomless regret and sorrow.

Abby's world slowly went dark.

25

Finding Solace

They always started with the crosses... every dream did since. The three crosses nailed into the ground. They were his only respite in an otherwise bleak and perpetual existence. But did he really exist anymore? Or was he just a passenger of destiny, being summoned from the barren moonscape in order to seek restitution that would never come?

The moon indeed always hung low in his world—wherever he was. It was a dull light in a vesper sky. Quite beautiful, actually. If he wasn't drowning in eternal sorrow and torment, maybe he could learn to exist here. But existence was something he'd given up on a century ago. Now it was simply a ruthless operation every time he was summoned, and nothing more. There had to be an end to this, he just knew it. He could still *feel* them sometimes, *see* them, sense their presence. The love they'd shared in his mortal life had never dwindled. Surely this was a sign.

Blood had vigor, and it drew life: yet it seemed there never was enough.

***

Over the past three weeks, Abby had endured rigorous questioning by authorities concerning the night of the slayings but could not remember a single thing that had happened.

She'd been found lying on the grass near the slaughterhouse that night by the resident of the farmhouse next door. Tucked into a fetal position, Abby had been shaking and mumbling. The Good Samaritan had assisted her to his home and called the authorities.

Memories of the cookout, their lake swim, the ghost stories told around the fire... those were still fresh in her mind. *Good* memories were all that remained, and maybe that was for the best. After being told what had happened to her friends that night (and God—Ben!), she secretly cherished not remembering having experienced that living nightmare.

"The Clatter Man..."

Those three words danced from Abby's lips as she sat in the comfort of her own bedroom, trying to unravel what happened that night.

THE CLATTER MAN

She felt so alone now: isolated and alone. The town was buzzing about the recent murders, and stepping outside only ensured she'd be stared at as some defective freak. Though her innocence had been proven, the sight of her still seemed to rile up outrage in others.

She *couldn't* have done those things. What were people *thinking*? But blaming her made it easy. The reality of it all was incomprehensible.

Her dreams since that night, though. They'd been so vivid—she could almost feel the cool air fill her lungs, and their soft skin under his rough fingers was divine. Anna, and the twins. She had felt his wife's tender cheeks as he caressed them and experienced the tranquil bliss that radiated warmth when hugging his two kids. Pure magic! And he knew she was there; she could sense it.

How could this be him? How could this absolute love and devotion exist within something so immensely vile? Abby's brow wrinkled in concentration as she tried to make sense of this, yet bewilderment lingered. There was something she was missing. An undeniable connection to his family still existed after all these years. The soft chime of her mom's voice calling from downstairs was a thankful distraction from exhausting rumination.

"Abby, sweetheart. Someone's here to see you!"

The lilt in her voice was unmistakable. Was it... could it be? But it had only been three weeks! Her heart fluttered—she *really* needed him right now. Jumping from her bed, Abby rushed down the stairs, almost tripping from sheer excitement.

There he was, standing just inside the doorway. The hazy sunlight filtering through the screen door bathed him in such a celestial glow, she began to weep.

"Dustin!"

Abby reached out to him with open arms, ready to deliver a big bear hug.

"Oh, easy there!" Dustin quipped, lifting his arms in defense with palms facing her. "Still healing, you know. Just... go easy on that hug."

"Oh my God." Abby laughed, wiping away tears of joy with the back of her hands. "Of course, I... I'm just so happy to *see* you!"

Abby looked up into those kind, hazel eyes; then she tilted her head in admiration. Lifting her hand up, she ran long fingers through his soft, wavy locks. As Dustin grinned, those dimples graced his cheeks, as did a splash of rouge.

"I can't..." She placed a hand softly against his stomach. "How did you *survive* that? And what are you *doing* here? I could have driven to see *you*, ya know. Just wasn't sure when you were gonna be up for it."

Shaking his head, he looked to the floor, then back to meet her gaze. "I'm fine. Still healing is all, but I'll be okay. Wound isn't that deep. And, dunno." His eyes began to glass over now. "You must be my good luck charm."

With a soft chuckle, Abby leaned in, wrapping her arms around him and resting her head against his chest... careful to be gentle. And when his arms embraced her, it felt warm. Loving. *Right.*

26

AT LAST

"So... you really can't remember *anything* from that night?" Dustin asked, peering at Abby incredulously.

They were both sitting on Abby's favorite couch in the sunroom. Her parents bought it when she was a kid. The soft moss-colored fabric contrasted so well with the cheerful yellow walls. And when the sun was setting, as it was now, the beams of light cast the room in golden hues. Fairy tale vibes.

"I mean..." She looked down at her crossed legs, taking in a deep breath before meeting his gaze again. "*No.* I remember arriving at the cabin, the cookout, us hanging out on the patio. But not a *thing* about the..." Sniffling, she hung her head down, and a fresh tear splattered onto the hardwood floor. It reminded her of her life now—once all together, these days it existed in fragments scattered about. She hadn't the slightest idea of how to piece them together, and simply lived moment to moment. Dustin leaned over the best he could, wincing from the pain of his healing wound, and rubbed her back.

"It's okay," he cooed. "Really... it's a blessing you don't remember a thing about it. Was a goddamn nightmare. Like, a real-life horror movie. And I..." He stifled a cry, then looked at her with glassy eyes. "I really thought I was a goner, you know? That *thing*. Pure evil, man. Pure. Fucking. Evil."

There was a pause as Abby took a deep breath, exhaling slowly while she considered her next words.

"I've had these dreams lately, and... I just know it's him, the Clatter Man. They're visions. Like—*memories*. Him and his family. And it's weird, because. Well, his wife. She looks so much like *me*. In a really weird way."

"Do you—" Dustin's brow creased and he lowered his gaze, lifting a fist to his lips in deep contemplation.

"What?" Abby asked.

"Well, do you... do you think *he* did this? The Clatter Man? Do you think he, like, wanted to *protect* you or something? Because..." Dustin leaned back, opening his arms wide. "Not to be a dick or anything, but there's literally *no* reason you should be here right now other than that. Somehow, I survived that goddamn *meat* cleaver. But *you*? You were fair game after that, and look at ya." He showcased her with his hands. "Hardly a scratch on you."

"I..." Abby blinked with confusion. "I mean, *maybe*? That sounds kinda crazy, though, doesn't it?"

"No more crazy than you being here, right now, pretty much unscathed." He shrugged his shoulders. "You know me, I don't shit around. I mean"—he chuckled—"seriously, this is kinda..." He cocked his head, then squinted briefly before peering at her with scrutiny. "Do you think you can maybe... get *through* to him somehow? Like, you know, *talk* to him? In your dreams, I mean. You've seen ghosts before, so maybe this is some kind of *sign*, you know? Familiar territory."

"Pfft... what?" Abby scoffed. "What do you *mean*, 'talk to him'?"

"*You* know. Like, convince him to *stop* or something. Try to get something out of him. Maybe..." Dustin's eyes lit up as he placed both palms on Abby's cheeks. "Maybe you can put an end to this, once and for all. He'll *listen* to you!"

"Um." Abby rubbed her arms, eyeing Dustin with skepticism. "This guy has been doing this shit since, like, the eighteen hundreds. I don't think I'm gonna be the one to *stop* him."

Dustin inhaled long and deep, letting his shoulders heave and fall. Nodding his head, he puckered his lips, then attempted to lean forward and place his forearms on his thighs. Wincing in pain, he sat up straight again, sighing in frustration. "Still takes getting used to, not being able to lean forward or having a hell of a time trying to laugh. Kinda my signature thing, you know? Laughter." Shrugging his shoulders, he smirked at Abby, and she softened under those gentle eyes.

All Dustin wanted to do right now was take Abby's pain away, just absorb it all. After a brief silence, he spoke again. "How you holdin' up? You must miss Ben and Val like crazy."

"Yeah, it's... I mean, I've accepted it now. Still fucking hurts, though."

"I know," Dustin said softly, reaching for her hand. "He was one helluva guy."

Abby leaned her head toward him, to which Dustin raised his arm so she could sink into his embrace. Her hair smelled of vanilla and strawberries—delicious and sweet. He felt a flutter in his stomach, and a smile spread across his face. Lifting his forearm, he gently caressed her hair, thinking about that night in the car. And somehow, he felt Ben's approval. Somehow, he felt his bud would be okay with this.

Closing her eyes, Abby relished in Dustin's warmth as he ran his fingers through her hair. Something was happening here, she felt: desire. To be held, to be loved, to laugh, to *kiss.*

Raising her head from Dustin's shoulder, Abby looked into his eyes. They were so kind, and the hazy afternoon sunlight filtering through the windows lit up his striking hazel irises. When his eyes turned up at the ends, those adorable dimples reappearing, Abby leaned in. Placing her fingertips on his chin, she pressed her lips against his. Dustin's eyes grew wide in surprise as his body tensed up, but he quickly softened to her touch. Placing his hand gently on her cheek, he kissed her soft and pure. It was delicate and sweet—and as the tears streamed down their cheeks and along their lips, they found release in a bout of passion. A gentle kiss turned into wanting, needing, yearning.

When their lips parted and they sat facing each other again, she realized what had been there all along: a deep attraction and understanding.

27

AGAINST ALL ODDS

Abby furrowed her brow as she drove on, contemplating their decision. It felt so rushed, and she wondered if they'd both acted in haste. What the hell were they *thinking*?

It had to be dealt with, though. Sure, they could move on and leave this all behind them. The killer would never be found, and it would remain an open case. But that would mean more innocent blood would be shed.

Besides, it was too late now—no going back.

She was only minutes away from Dustin's house. After mulling over their conversation a couple days ago, she'd called him up and told him she'd do it: She would attempt to face the Clatter Man in her dreams and end this.

He was sitting on the front wraparound porch of his house when she arrived, looking calm as ever. He was a bit of an old soul at times, and it was refreshing.

Walking up to the porch, that adorable smile of his lit up and he stood to greet her.

"Hey, beautiful."

"Hey, yourself," Abby replied, lifting her head to kiss him. He wrapped his arms around the small of her back, glowing at her now, then leaned down to kiss her. She then placed her head against his chest, wrapping her arms around him as well. His heart beat slow and rhythmic.

"So..."

"What?" Dustin asked, with a light chuckle.

"Do you really think this is possible?"

He loosened his embrace and gazed down at her. "Well... *Yeah. I do.*"

"But I've never tried to interact with him. I mean, I'm *there*. I experience every memory with him, but... I mean, *think* about it. What if he does some Freddy Krueger shit on me?"

"What, like kill you in your *dream*?" Dustin laughed, then winced as he put a hand to his back. "I'm not laughing *at* you," he insisted. "Just, I mean. Goddamn brilliant movie." He caught her questionable stare.

Shrugging her shoulders, she raised her arms, palms up, waiting for an answer. When she received just a giggle, she slapped him playfully on the arm.

"Ow!" Dustin snickered, rubbing his arm in jest. "And no. I'll be right here with you. He tries anything, I'll wake you up."

Abby donned a coy smile, pointing a finger at him. "You *better*, mister!" Then, pausing, she frowned in concern. "When I saw Regina's ghost that night, she kept on saying she should have listened. Maybe that's my cue? Maybe that's how I get *through* to him, you know? Make him really listen to me. I mean..." Abby looked to the ground, wringing her hands together. "...maybe this really is all happening for a reason, the fact that I look so much like his wife."

Dustin nodded, then tilted his head and shrugged. "Only one way to find out."

"I'm serious about that Freddy shit, though," Abby snapped. "You hear me moan or see me kick, scream, *anything*... wake me up, okay?"

"Deal." Dustin reached his hand out, and they shook on it.

A little weed had softened tense nerves as a sapphire evening sky revealed itself. The stars were beautiful that night, not a cloud in sight. Dustin took a puff of the joint, then handed it to Abby. They were sitting on the steps of his deck, gazing at the dark skyline.

Abby took the last hit of the joint, and after she exhaled a plume of smoke into the air and watched it rise to the sparkling canopy above, she spoke.

"To Ben, Jamie, and Val."

Dustin nodded his head in agreement, the sentiment ushering in the task at hand.

"You think they're up there, in the stars?" Abby asked.

"I'd like to think so," Dustin replied, marveling at the brilliant night sky. "Ben is the North Star, guiding the way. And Jamie's that star right next to the North Star. See?" He pointed above and Abby rested her head on his shoulder, lifting her gaze to where he was pointing. "And that star that's kinda spazzin' out right now, flickering and shit, that's Val."

"*Stop* it!" Abby laughed, sitting up and giving him a playful slap.

Dustin snickered, then his eyes drooped and the smile left his lips. He gazed at her, and she could see the melancholy in his expression.

"It's just you and *me* now, isn't it?"

"Just you and me," Abby whispered, gently placing her hand on his.

"Yeah," he sniffled, rubbing his nose with the back of his other hand as memories of Ben, Val, and Jamie played in his mind. Then, sitting up straight, he stared at her, resolute, and nodded.

"Let's get this motherfucker."

***

Dustin was fighting off sleep with increasingly tired, heavy eyes. After much arguing, he'd agreed to sleep in bed with her and not on their blow-up mattress. The more he pushed back on it, the more adorable he became. And though he wasn't doing it on purpose, Abby couldn't help being smitten by his chivalry.

As his eyes fluttered, losing against the progression of incoming slumber, Abby stayed alert and fraught. Her body would surely communicate struggle, even in a dream state. Wouldn't it?

Once he was fast asleep, his slow breathing a litany of calm, she began to fight her own slumber. Weary eyelids brought in the terrifying darkness that would soon envelop her—and though she knew she had to succumb to it, her body still fought in the form of taut muscles and a racing mind.

Resting a hand on Dustin's arm, Abby breathed in and out in slow, intentional breaths. As the storm raging in her mind began to quiet, so too did her body. Muddled unease ceased its incessant scratching and a calm clarity swept over her now, releasing all tension. She sunk into this deep and welcoming relaxation.

Then, looking one more time at his peaceful face, Abby closed her eyes and gave in to the blackness.

28

Forlorn

The air was pungent with sweat and remorse. Low-hanging clouds crawled across a gray sky that hung damp with death and decay. He was there, as she most often saw him, standing in front of the three wooden crosses nailed into the ground.

Abby could discern the slight rise and dip of hulking shoulders as he stared at the knotted wood, and she gasped amidst a sudden jolt of vulnerability, the frigid air cooling her lungs. It seemed he heard her; his body leaned slightly, then stilled.

Wake up, wake up, wake up!

Abby's heartbeat quickened as her muscles tightened in fear. Despite every fiber in her being wanting to wake up from this, she stayed here... in the dark abyss. An idea driven by confidence and justification thinned and scattered like ash across the sullen landscape. A fathomless void filled where surety had once been, and all that could be felt now was buckling anguish.

"Now you feel what I feel. What I have felt for over a *century*!" The hoarse voice cut its way into the atmosphere, resounding all around her.

Abby winced as the anguish she felt turned into torment and began to compress her small frame. She craned her neck, struggling to move, but to no avail—claustrophobia kicked in as the sky began to darken and the vice grip on her body tightened.

"Don't fight it... already tried that. It's like a big snake. More you struggle, the more it crushes you."

"You don't..." Abby began, squeezing the words out from within. "...you don't have to do this anymore. You won't... you won't get them back."

"Oh, but my *dear*. Yes, I will. That is where you're wrong."

The Clatter Man turned around now, and the maimed face Abby had seen before was replaced with a handsome appearance. A brittle beard framed a strong jawline, and orbs that had once been shallow pits had been replaced with kind brown eyes. Though they hung with sorrow, there was still that immense love. She could feel it now—*see* it.

"I have always felt you visit me. You have her face... her pure heart." He placed his large hand on her sternum as he said this, and Abby's heartbeat obediently returned to a normal pace. "I've never seen such a *resemblance* before."

Tears clouded her vision as Abby pleaded with him. "Anna would not want you to keep killing. You *know* that."

He cocked his head and lifted a weathered hand to her face, running coarse fingers along her sleek jawline. Mesmerized by his warm affection, Abby softened... and so did the fixed pressure on her body. His large, brown eyes radiated warmth and protection, and she began to feel herself succumb to this confusing, soothing aura of his.

"There she is. My lovely, dearest Anna. What a cruel world, to smother your light so soon. So... spiteful."

The gentleness in his expression faded now as it turned scornful and his skin began to melt, resembling dripping candle wax. Fluid-filled blisters erupted across his visage in blotchy, swollen masses. One by one, they started to pop, revealing the raw and tender flesh underneath. Clear fluid seeped from the open wounds, which transformed from shades of ripe red to sickly brown. Smooth and taut skin had become replaced by a map of charred tissue, revealing sinewy muscles and tendons beneath that squirmed within, and a vicious smile spread across his countenance. His soft brown eyes had lost their color and all lucidity disappeared, replaced by hollow pits. A voice boomed from this macabre figure now standing before her.

"Did you see not what they *did* to me? Did you not see the *wrath*?"

Abby shook her head, lips quivering with a lost thought hoping to verbalize, but nothing came out. The pressure on her grew stronger once more, and the compression impacted her breathing.

"Do you want to know what it feels like to be burned alive? To have your organs burned while you sit there, unable to move, only able to feel *every* single affliction?"

Lifting her chin up, Abby's eyes grew wide and her mouth quivered, trying to find the strength to speak.

"Yes, that's it. I see the horror in your face now. Anna... don't you understand? Look." He pointed with a charred finger to the three crosses. "Can't you *see*? Every time I *kill*, the crosses become smaller. Every time blood is shed, I get closer to having you, Patrick, and Susie back. When the crosses are no more, you will be with me again. The four of us... we will be together."

"The... but I don't see..." Abby managed to sputter.

"*Surely* you see how your cross has reduced in size. Surely that is unmistakable."

Abby looked to the crosses again, breathing in thin gasps, but saw no difference in size. They were all identical, not one smaller than the rest.

"This... this isn't..."

"*Each* kill, Anna. Each kill brings us closer together again. So I will keep on killing, until I get you back. No matter how long it takes. We will be back together again, forever."

"But I don't think... the crosses are not getting smaller. Don't you *see*? They're all the same size. This isn't..." Her eyes fell on the fiery bursts that his eyes had transformed into again, now glowing a dark red. Terrified, she still pressed forward with her next words.

"You can't get your family back."

A chill fell upon her as a cool breeze brushed against her skin, prickling her flesh. He lowered his head, and a shallow moan rumbled from within his core. It grew ever so louder, and as the sound crescendoed to a roar, the earth beneath her feet began to crumble away. Suspended in the air, she looked at him, transfixed in front of her. Roots extended from the bottoms of the crosses, running down into the dark void below. They glowed red and pulsated with her heartbeat.

"More blood. I need more blood. Yours will do just fine."

His hand flew out to her, thick fingers seeking the soft flesh of her neck—

"Abby! *Abby!*" Dustin was patting her cheek when her eyes fluttered open.

In an instant, she shot up; chest heaving, she panicked and surveyed her surroundings. Dustin's face flew by in a blur as she scanned the entire room, shaking her head in shock. His gentle voice grounded her.

"You were kicking and moaning, so I did what I could to wake you up. Sorry about that hard slap." He cringed.

The ache in her left cheek throbbed, and she placed a palm to her warm jawline.

"You… you're okay?" he asked. Then, he nodded. "You look okay. But holy shit, I think he was about to get you!"

Her lips trembled as the words struggled to come forth. Dustin tilted his head and stared at her with deep concern. "What is it?"

"I didn't… I couldn't stop him. Dustin, I couldn't stop him—he'll never stop, because it will never be *enough*!" She shook her head in despair as the full realization of his wretched plight took hold.

"He's a tortured soul," Abby whispered, staring into nothingness. "Tortured souls never rest."

Epilogue

Dustin glanced at Abby in the passenger seat as he drove along. She was gazing ahead as the road lumbered on, and her countenance was grave. Every so often, the grief would kick in. It was inevitable.

Smiling, Abby looked into his eyes and gently placed her palm on his chest. His stomach had gotten a lot smaller in the year after that fatal night, but he still did love wearing those ridiculous Hawaiian shirts. Ridiculously cute, in her opinion.

In the year that had followed, they'd become extremely close. At first, just having each other to lean on had been a godsend. But she adored his tenderness, affection, and perfectly timed humor. And yes, there were glints of Ben in him, too. Letting down her walls completely had been easy, and their initial spark had evolved into what it was today—a deep love for each other.

He slowed his car down as they approached a stoplight, and while she stared at him with those gorgeous blue-gray eyes he loved to get lost in, a car engine roared next to her.

Looking to her right, Abby saw a boy and a girl in a Chevy Blazer. The boy was driving, and revving the engine now as both him and the girl goaded Dustin on. But the boy had a meat cleaver lodged into his skull, and blood was trickling down his forehead as he sported a nasty grin. Closing her eyes, she shook her head, then looked back at the Blazer. The cleaver was gone, and there was no blood. Still that same sick grin, though.

"You okay?" Dustin asked, placing his hand on her thigh.

Oh, God—it's happening again, Abby thought. Turning to Dustin, she smiled and sighed. "I... I'm fine. All good."

The engine of the Blazer next to them revved on, with the crass hoots and hollers continuing. Abby's face grew flush with annoyance; the red light was lasting excruciatingly long.

Dustin smirked at the boy and girl in the Blazer as he lowered his head and nodded, touching the brim of his ball cap while revving the engine of his brand-new Toyota Supra.

Abby looked at him and grinned wide, biting her lower lip. "Smoke 'em, babe."

And when the light turned green, he peeled out, laughing as Abby cheered in exaltation.

***

The sun had just set below the horizon, painting the sky in a flurry of colorful magic as the Blazer made a right onto Lakeside Drive. The owners of Reeves Cabin had finally decided to open it up again for guests due to their insatiable curiosity. It stood a dark omen now on the far side of the lake.

Will removed a hand from the steering wheel to turn the volume down as they rounded the bend to the cabin, lowering Radiohead's melodic haze. Sandy sat in the front passenger seat, her bare feet on the dashboard, drumming her toes.

"So this is the place, huh," Sandy said. "Where it all went down a year ago."

"This is the *place*," Will replied.

"Do you think it's really *real*, though? I mean, *c'mon*," Justine said from the backseat, rolling her eyes. "Probably just some madman on a killing spree." She glanced at Maggie, who sat in between her and Trent, and noticed her friend's fraught demeanor. Maggie's brows were knitted and she was clenching her thighs.

"I don't know," Trent replied. "But we've all heard the stories... I mean, that dude on the bed was flat-out *massacred*. And the slaughterhouse death? That can't be a coincidence."

Maggie rubbed her arms, trying to quell the budding goosebumps. "I never even wanted to come here, guys. I mean, *look* at this place. It's freaky."

Will shifted the Blazer into park as they pulled into the gravel driveway. "Well, freaky is *good*. Freaky means we'll see some *ghosts*."

Sandy peered at Will, then their three friends in the back seat. "Leave the conjuring to me, I heard how it's done. Just a small slice on the finger, no biggie."

Maggie lowered her head and winced, the sense of unease growing stronger now. She hoped Justine was right.

"Oh, Maggie." Justine playfully elbowed her friend in the side, as if on cue. "You're too much of a scaredy cat. No monster's gonna chop us up!"

As they began to unpack and bring their bags into the cabin, Maggie stopped short of the front door. She felt a slight chill brush her back amid the warm August breeze and turned around, but nothing was there. Only the calm stillness of the lake and the buzzing cadence of crickets. But then, squinting, she discerned a figure standing under a tree at the top of the embankment. It was a girl about their age with pallid skin and long, black hair. Her powerful stare hit Maggie so viscerally that, for a second, she couldn't find her breath.

With a slow, dull shake of her head, the figure mouthed the word "No." Maggie blinked in bewilderment a few times, and then the girl was gone. Trembling, she wondered if it was just her imagination playing tricks—a full moon did hang in the evening sky.

After a minute or two, she shrugged her shoulders, reckoning the shadows were simply playing tricks on her. Humming a sweet tune, Maggie walked through the front door to join her friends.

It was silly... the Clatter Man was just an urban legend.

Afterword

I began writing *The Clatter Man* while I was finalizing my previous horror novella, *Death Cult*. I've always loved the cabin trope in horror, when you have a group of people setting off to a remote cabin where all hell breaks loose. It's fun, it's bloody, and the isolation works so effectively to elevate panic and tension.

The urban legend aspect was born from my fascination with urban legends during my childhood in Ohio. There is one I distinctly remember, called Crybaby Bridge. According to this legend, if you parked your vehicle on a particular bridge and left the engine idling, you would hear the distant cries of a baby rising up from the murky depths below. Did my friends and I ever try this? You betcha!

In fact, I can still clearly remember sitting in my car with my three best friends at twilight, just listening to the soft rumble of the engine as our eyes darted back and forth in nervous anticipation. Did we think we heard cries? Of course! Because when it comes to horror, your mind likes to play tricks on you. It's part of the fun, and part of the fright! The unknown sparks up curiosity and fear, which are both at the heart of many urban legends. Sure, it could be complete hearsay... but what if it isn't?

I chose Pennsylvania as the location for the cabin because it's a beautiful state filled with lakes and wooded areas. You want isolation? There's lots of it! Having grown up in Ohio, I visited Pennsylvania often, so it was easy for me to picture this location in my mind. A lakeside cabin rental my family and I booked a few years ago in Pennsylvania helped even more as inspiration for this story. Interestingly enough, many consider it a haunted state as well—even better!

Before I began writing *The Clatter Man*, I already knew Reeves Cabin was going to be an A-Frame. There was an A-frame cabin at the top of the street I grew up on, and I just loved admiring it when driving or walking by. The sweeping design was so beautiful, and of course the glass facade was gorgeous! It's such a unique style, and the facade offered the perfect display for Val's demise as well. Though horrific, I wanted to add a sense of beauty with the slow-motion twinkling of glass shards as her body broke through. This scene almost has a cinematic quality to it.

The origin of the Clatter Man was fleshed out midway through writing this book, and I began creating it right after the campfire scene. I knew I wanted his character to hail back to the 1800s (this adds a further layer of mystery and intrigue), and the slaughterhouse backstory just fit. This way I could also give him that wicked hook! But there's a love story involved as well. I enjoy when villains are imbued with qualities that evoke sympathy, because this adds further complexity to a story. Sure, the Clatter Man is slicing and dicing up those who summon him up, but he also feels the more blood shed the closer he gets to having his family back.

It's horror mixed with sorrow, a combination I find compelling. Abby is able to tap into the humanity the Clatter Man still possesses, and through this connection we are able to experience glints of his mortal life.

The fun mix of characters in this story helps to create lively banter among them, and also showcases their close friendships well before the chaos ensues. The cookout scene is one of my favorites, because it paints them all in such a playful light, yet also creates a false sense of security. And who doesn't love a summer barbecue?

Though Abby is the main character, when Dustin enters the scene he becomes another pivotal character. I love how he enters this story, smoking a joint and just ready to have a good time. This is such a defining character trait of his, and I wanted his introduction to lead with this vibe. He offers some comedic relief as well along with Val and Jamie, while Ben is the most stalwart of them all.

Abby's character is inherently the voice of caution and reason, relying on her past experiences and intuition. And though she is more timid in the beginning, as the story unfolds we see her gain confidence and find her footing. At the end of this story, Abby discovers survival instincts and strength she never knew she had, especially in confronting the Clatter Man in the abandoned slaughterhouse and her dream.

When I first began writing *The Clatter Man*, the romance existed solely between Abby and Ben. But Dustin was such a lovable character (and so good for Abby), that I changed the narrative to create the love triangle that exists between the three of them. And of course, I wanted to add that little twist in the end when he arrives at Abby's door. He represents the carefree that left her life when her dad died. And when I envisioned him in my head, those Hawaiian shirts just clicked.

Though the romance in this story exists first within the love triangle, we see it begin to materialize in the way the Clatter Man sees Abby. She is his Anna, alive and well. I enjoyed using this connection to weave their stories together.

Abby's parents are written as tributes to my parents, both of whom I lost in 2020. I remember my mom always cozying up in the mornings with her coffee and newspaper in hand while the news played in the background. She was so loving, tender, and kind. Being the youngest of three (and the only girl), my dad used to always call me his favorite daughter. You can imagine the shock this drew from strangers when we were out and about! But, of course, we always explained the inside joke. Hence the mug that Abby grabs on her way out. And one of my dad's favorite sayings was, "It is what it is." He used to always say this in a singsong tune as well.

I hope readers of *Death Cult* enjoyed that little easter egg in the beginning, too!

The idea of the wind chimes came to me spontaneously. I wanted something fervid to happen as Chuck Blackthorne's life was taken, and the sound of wind chimes rattling all over town as he perished seemed perfect and incredibly ominous. He loved his family fiercely, and they loved him just as much in return, thus the wind chimes embodying their mournful wails. One of my best friends had gifted me wind chimes with beautiful inscriptions after my parents passed away, and oddly enough I did not connect this until after I'd finished writing the Clatter Man's backstory. The subconscious works in mysterious ways, doesn't it?

I don't come up with titles for my books until I finish them, so after I'd finished this story I went straight to his backstory to brainstorm title ideas. Once I ruminated over the sound of wind chimes, I chose *The Clatter Man*. It just fit so well—unique, mysterious, and unsettling.

Ah yes, and those cars Dustin drives... Senior year of high school and into college, my friends and I used to frequent classic car shows. We loved admiring the older models with their unique designs. And yet, there was often a small group of modern cars parked not far from the older models. There was almost always a Chevy Impala SS and a Toyota Supra (usually a turbo). These are two of my very favorite models from the '90s, hence why I included them in the story. Both cars were fast, had such sleek designs, and definitely got you the hell outta dodge!

Horror should be scary, but it should also be fun! By adding humor and romance to this story, I was able to lighten the mood and balance out the tension throughout. What I also love about horror is the what-if factor. Sure, this can be applied to any genre. But when applied to horror, it can be deadly. And urban legends are a big what-if.

I hope you enjoyed reading *The Clatter Man*, and thank you so much for your support. Please consider leaving a review or rating—these are so important for self-published authors such as myself because they help our work get noticed and allow us to continue sharing our stories.

Take care, Dear Reader… and careful with those urban legends.

Also by

Also by Janelle Schiecke
Death Cult
Ghost Room

ABOUT THE AUTHOR

Janelle Schiecke lives with her husband, her son, and their two cats. This is her third self-published book, and she has always reveled in horror and everything spooky.

Though she began her career editing trade magazines and nonfiction, she now enjoys delivering scares to fellow horror and paranormal fans with the stories she writes.

When she is not working on that next story, Janelle enjoys spending time with her family and friends, catching up on the latest streaming series and movies, and planning her next family travel adventure.

You can follow Janelle on her social media accounts below:

Twitter/X: https://x.com/J_Schiecke

Instagram: https://www.instagram.com/janelle.schiecke

Goodreads: https://www.goodreads.com/author/show/42431965.Janelle_Schiecke

For more information, including upcoming books, feel free to visit: https://www.janelleschiecke.com/